Pilar Sinquemani

Chronicles of a divorcee

SINGULAR
PUBLISING LLC

Chronicles of a Divorcee
First Edition by Singular Publishing Group LLC. 2019
Copyright © 2019 by María Pilar Rodríguez Sinquemani
All rights reserved, including the rights of reproduction in whole or in part in any form.

psinquemani@singularpublishingllc.com
Published by Singular Publishing Group LLC.

The cataloging information in this publication is available in the Library of Congress. United States of America.

ISBN-978-1-947687-01-1

Design: Olivieri Guadalupe
Production: Singular Publishing LLC

Printed in the United States of America.

Preface

We are but the memories we make.

P. Sinquemani

Chapter 1

Jacqueline rushed through the crowded streets of New York City. The frenzy of rush hour pounded in her head, and its swarming sounds served only to add more stress to her already troubled mood. She crossed the intersection and raised the collar of her mink coat, protecting herself from a sudden slap of frigid air.

Jacqueline couldn't have cared less about parties or socializing with friends. However, on that Thursday night, she needed to unload her frustrations on anyone kind enough to listen. She lived in the heart of the city and found it convenient to arrange a date at the St. Regis hotel with her friend Ariana.

After a short walk, Jacqueline approached the revolving doors that granted entry to the luxurious building. The doorman stepped to the side. "Good evening, ma'am," he said.

Jacqueline glanced at him absently as she shuffled her feet on the red carpeted walkway. "Good evening," she whispered with a distracted smile.

She maneuvered through the packed-to-the-brim lobby. People were gathered in groups, mostly men of good breeding—or so they seemed—dressed in dark suits. Some talked among themselves, while others seemed bored and stood, zombie-like, holding their drinks and sipping almost imperceptibly.

The St. Regis hotel, with its traditional French decor, was considered by many to be one of the best in the city. It exuded an air of sophistication, and the impeccable service made it a favorite spot for businessmen and important politicians. The private meeting rooms were favored for hosting medical conferences and multinational corporations.

Jacqueline wove her way through, sidestepping the havoc and admiring the decorative crown moldings that stood out in the reflections of the crystal chandeliers. Once at the entrance of the hotel bar, she scanned the room and realized that Ariana had not yet arrived. She felt uneasy being alone in this type of place but was determined not to let her insecurities show. She walked to the only open barstool and sat down, trying to convey the confidence she lacked.

Unlike the lobby, the hotel bar had a more inviting atmosphere. The place was filled with young professionals talking among themselves and laughing occasionally at their own jokes, giving the space a more relaxed ambiance.

Jacqueline approached the bar, and the bartender noticed her right away. "Good evening, ma'am. What can I get for you?"

"A glass of wine, please."

"White or red?"

"Red. Cabernet," she said, removing her black leather gloves.

"Would you like to start a tab?"

"No. I'm waiting for someone," she said, handing him her credit card. He took it, briefly distracted by the glittering bracelet dangling from her wrist.

Sensing a presence behind her, Jacqueline looked over her shoulder. She wasn't thrilled to see a tall man smiling coyly at her. Their eyes met briefly, and she glared at him, unimpressed. From that short distance, she could see that his teeth were dazzling white, perhaps due to their contrast with his dark skin. The man was well dressed in a dark blue suit, red striped tie, and gold cufflinks.

Those who knew Jacqueline praised her rather old- fashioned manners. Chatting in bars with strangers was not her thing. She took off her coat, laid it over the barstool, and saw the man walk straight to her side of the bar, leaning casually only inches away from her.

"I'll have a scotch on the rocks," he said to the bartender.

"Right away, sir."

Jacqueline leaned to the opposite side, her discomfort evident. The man was oblivious to Jacqueline's annoyance, and she wondered what about her had captured his attention.

"It looks like you had a hard day," he said. "Too much work?"

"I don't work," she said, feigning disinterest.

"Are you from out of town?" he asked, and she smiled, letting her guard down almost immediately.

"No, I live two blocks away."

"Oh, I see. This seems like a nice neighborhood," he said, trying to prolong the small talk.

"I would rather live in Soho," Jacqueline said. "It's a little boring here; nothing happens."

"Too quiet an area for you, huh?" he said, holding out his hand. "My name is William. William Harron."

"Nothing is ever too quiet in New York City," she replied as she extended her hand politely. "Jacqueline Kingsley. Before you get any ideas, I don't go out to bars to meet anyone. I'm married with children," she added haughtily, hoping to scare him away. However, the apparent kindness in his eyes and the warmth in his smile made her feel guilty for answering with forced arrogance. William was not offended by her abrasiveness and even found her bluntness charming. He laughed.

"Well . . . I wasn't trying to make a move on you, merely being friendly," he said nonchalantly. "I just got out of a medical conference here at the hotel. Today was the last day."

Jacqueline was in dire need of a connection with the world. She felt empty in her loveless marriage, starved for attention, and it showed.

"Don't you have some kind of closing dinner? When the conference is over, I mean?"

"Yes, sometimes," he said. "But I'm not in the mood to mingle tonight. I haven't been sleeping well lately. I figured a drink before bed would be a good idea."

"Warm milk is usually a better remedy for insomnia, I think. But then again, you're the doctor. You should know," said Jacqueline, and he agreed with a smile.

"Perhaps insomnia is not the right word. Frequent jet lag would be a better term," he said.

William was not particularly shy, but Jacqueline found him socially awkward. He wore hideous glasses so thick they made his eyes look like tiny peas.

"Do you work in the city?" she asked.

"I live in New Jersey. I have my practice there."

"My brother-in-law is a doctor, and he lived in New Jersey as well but moved with my sister to Switzerland. They just opened a first-class facility for research on obesity or something like that."

"That's quite a change of work."

"Yes," she agreed, "but he's about to retire and they always wanted to set up some kind of rehab for people with food addictions. There are not many here in the US since the main focus seems to be on research to develop meds and a quick fix."

"Why not here? I'm sure there's a great demand for that here as well," he asked, seeming genuinely curious. Jacqueline explained that her brother-in-law had a group of investors in Geneva who were happy to invest in the development of the facility and the project. William seemed impressed.

Jacqueline and William talked for a while about the city. They shared stories about countries they had traveled to and were surprised to find they had been to many of the same places. William had a busy life, and his trips had been mainly business-related. Jacqueline suggested some well-known restaurants in the city and warned him about some popular places she found overrated. Instead, she suggested a few local restaurants she considered better and less expensive.

William talked about his life. He had gotten married at a young age and had four boys. During his early years, he had been consumed with school. It was evident to Jacqueline that for William, the nightlife had been almost nonexistent. He had spent most days studying for long hours, and after getting married, children came faster than he had planned. Then, his nightlife had been about building his career.

Jacqueline received a text from Ariana, who had unexpectedly changed plans and was now waiting for her at the rooftop restaurant of the Peninsula Hotel.

Jacqueline wished William a good evening, and he thanked her for the restaurant recommendations. As she was about to pay, he intervened.

"I got it. Please. It's the least I can do," he insisted. "You saved me from a lonely night at the bar."

This was the first time Jacqueline had spent a pleasant time chatting with a stranger at a social outing without her husband, Phil. They hardly went anywhere together anymore.

William had managed to help her forget the sorrowful life she lived inside her marriage, if only for a short time. He helped her get into her coat, and she smiled.

"William, if you like, next time you're in town, perhaps we can meet for coffee or even have dinner at one of those restaurants I mentioned," she offered shyly and was shocked at her own audacity. She didn't mean much by it and was immediately concerned that she would come off as aggressively pursuing something more than mere friendship.

"I would love that," he said. They exchanged numbers.

By the time she stepped out of the lobby, the rain had stopped. She walked just a block over to the Peninsula Hotel and went directly to the elevators. Once on the top floor, Jacqueline stepped out and suddenly felt someone grab her arm.

"Where do you think you're going in such a hurry?"

She turned to see Ariana, who laughed loud enough to make people turn and stare.

"You haven't changed a bit," Jacqueline said as they hugged.

Jacqueline and Ariana were as close as best friends could be, but they had not seen each other in nearly a year. That same week, they had spoken on the phone frequently and reconnected while giving each other much-needed support.

"Come! I already have a table over there," Ariana said, pulling Jacqueline closer to her.

"What happened to your friend Laurie? I thought she was coming," said Jacqueline.

"Laurie's a little shit. She wouldn't come because her husband would get pissed—can you imagine?"

"Really? But I thought her husband let her go out with her friends whenever—"

"Oh, please. She can't sneeze without his approval."

Jacqueline laughed. "I'm sure you're exaggerating."

"It's true! I'm not exaggerating. The poor woman lives like a criminal under house arrest! Anyway, they're going to Florida tomorrow. Something about an unexpected real estate deal her husband is closing on," said Ariana.

"How wonderful! Real estate is always a good business when you know what you're doing," said Jacqueline. In reality, she didn't know much of anything regarding business but felt compelled to mention it since Ariana had been in that business for over twenty-five years. The hostess offered the menus, and Jacqueline asked for the sommelier.

"When are you going to introduce me to your husband's business partners, Jacky?" asked Ariana. "They would be great for a few good listings, you know? Talk to Phil—"

"I don't know anyone selling anything, Ari," said Jacqueline, taking the wine list from the sommelier.

"That's okay if they don't wanna sell. They can always buy something! Real estate is the best investment! Especially in New York," Ariana said as she ran her long fingernails through her jet-black hair, ruffling her modern pixie. The stunning contrast between her dark hair and green eyes gave her an Elizabeth Taylor–like air.

"I don't know, Ari. I already told you I don't get to see Phil's friends as often as before. Phil and I barely even see each other lately."

"Can he at least talk to them? Referrals, hello?" Ariana insisted, and Jacqueline shook her head. She hoped to convince Ariana to let go of the idea. "You know Phil's affair has made our situation at home worse than ever. My life with him has been unbearable for months."

"I know, Jacky," said Ariana in a low voice. "I think he's about to ask for a divorce."

"Do you really think so?" asked Jacqueline, and Ariana nodded.

"Definitely. That's how men get when they're really into someone else."

"I know, but what can I do?" whispered Jacqueline.

Ariana stared at her. "Confront him!"

"And say what? That I've seen his text messages and emails?"

"That's exactly what you should say."

"And what if I make things worse by confronting him? What if he leaves? It's bad enough that he sleeps on the couch when he's home," said Jacqueline.

"He barely stays at home, Jacqueline; who are you kidding? It's just not right for your husband to spend only three nights a week at home."

"Do you think it's as serious as I think it is?"

"You have to make some sort of plan. I think what you've done today is spectacular," said Ariana with a broad smile. Jacqueline held her hand warmly.

"Going out tonight without him, right?" She sounded uncertain.

"He won't realize what a good thing he has until he thinks he's about to lose you. When Phil sees that you have a new attitude and couldn't care less about him, you just watch him kick that bimbo to the curb and come crawling back to you—I'm sure of it."

"I don't think it's that easy. I don't know what else to do. I'm running out of ideas," Jacqueline said, almost whispering, and Ariana leaned over.

"Men are not that complicated. They're like children. You have to keep them entertained, do something different from time to time— something new that takes them by surprise. Sometimes fighting for no reason works like a charm."

"Fighting for no reason?"

"Of course! Show him a few different personalities. That'll keep him entertained," she said jokingly and leaned in closer. "I think I overdid it with Carlos, and look at him now—gay after fifty . . ."

"Are you planning to divorce Carlos? Seriously?"

Ariana was silent for a few seconds as her face assumed a mournful stare. "Yes, and there's no turning back now. At my age, there's no point in pretending for appearances' sake. I couldn't stand it now if I tried. I finally get why we haven't had sex in years: He's gay!"

"I know your case is a little extreme, but a sexless marriage is not as uncommon as you might think. But gay—well, that's a deal-breaker for sure," said Jacqueline. They felt compelled to change the subject and talked about Ariana's new job opportunities in the city. Jacqueline talked about her children. The oldest wanted to go to a sleep-over summer camp, but for Jacqueline and Phil, having him away from home for any length of time was out of the question. Ariana ordered some appetizers and they shared memories from their past, laughing despite their problems at home.

Unlike Jacqueline, Ariana had grown up in a broken home. Shortly after her mother died, during her first year in college, she had met Carlos. After their first date, Carlos and Ariana were inseparable. Through the years, he had even helped Ariana build a decent real estate business, and with great effort they had managed to build a relatively comfortable life together.

Ariana had always acknowledged Carlos as a fatherly figure in her life and professed that he had given her all that she had missed during her younger years. Carlos was the rock she had leaned on in tough times and had given her the family she always dreamed of. Now, in her late forties, she prided herself on that certain degree of normalcy. Finding her husband in bed with her cousin Johnny had shattered everything that mattered to her overnight. Her drinking had spiraled out of control. She knew that most people didn't lose a mother to anorexia and a husband to a homosexual affair. She must be cursed, she thought.

"Jackie," said Ariana, "he's having an affair with my cousin!"

"I know, Ari. You told me. It's the last thing I ever expected, ever," said Jacqueline, placing her silverware on the empty dinner plate.

"Can you imagine? How awful! With a man! How can I forgive that?"

"There's no use, Ari. You can't. He's obviously not who you thought he was. It happens," said Jacqueline, shrugging. "Have you spoken to him since you left?"

Ariana stared back at her with a drawn face. "Hell, no! I did text him . . ." she said. "I left the house in total shock. Jacky! He's with a man!"

"It's probably better if you don't see him, at least for now. Have you spoken to Johnny at all?"

Ariana shook her head. "Can you believe that he got a restraining order against me? Ridiculous!"

"Really?" said Jacqueline in a sarcastic tone, and Ariana leaned forward.

"What?"

"Why are you surprised that he got a restraining order? I think I would've done the same after reading twenty-nine text messages threatening my life. Wouldn't you?"

"Oh, please. Give me a break, Jacqueline. I was drunk!"

"So what will you do?" Jacqueline asked.

"Same as always. I'll go to work and make money and gather up the pieces of what little dignity I have left," she said. "How was the St. Regis bar? I always find it too crowded for my taste."

"It was okay. I met someone."

Ariana slid her chair closer. "Someone? That sounds like something to me."

"He seemed a little too geeky for me. Even if I were single, I wouldn't look at him that way," said Jacqueline.

Ariana rolled her eyes and smiled. "Have you ever considered dating a woman?"

"God, Ari, you say the craziest things!"

"What do you know? Is he married or single?"

"I don't know, Ari. I didn't ask."

"Hmmm . . . what does he do?" asked Ariana, interested in every detail.

"He's a doctor."

"Oh! That's wonderful! I'm such a wreck these days; you just never know when I might need one," said Ariana in a serious tone. "If you're planning to mourn your dead marriage with a candlelight vigil, please let me know. I can always keep your doctor friend entertained."

"Stop it, Ari," said Jacqueline between laughs.

Ariana shrugged. "Why not? After seeing Carlos in bed with another man, any straight guy is a godsend!"

Jacqueline's housekeeper called, interrupting their conversation. Donna had been babysitting Jacqueline's children that night and was calling to tell Jacqueline she needed to go home. It was already after midnight, and she would have to catch the train soon. Her husband would be meeting her at the train station since she lived in a neighborhood near the roughest part of town. Jacqueline agreed and reassured her that she would be home shortly. The children were already asleep, and ten minutes without supervision wouldn't be so bad. Donna agreed and wished her good night.

Jacqueline paid the tab, and they grabbed their coats from the coatroom before rushing to the elevators. As they stepped out of the lobby, Ariana stumbled, and Jacqueline grabbed her arm to preserve her balance. Ariana had had way too much to drink, and Jacqueline felt uneasy about sending her home on her own as she eyed the pouring rain.

"Shit!" said Ariana. "Just my luck."

"Where did you park?" asked Jacqueline.

"I came on the train. Carlos kept the car."

"Good. I don't think driving would be a good idea for you right now anyway," said Jacqueline. After a few minutes passed with no vacant taxi in sight, she took out her phone. "I'll call Randy. Hopefully, he's close by."

"No, don't worry about it. I'll catch the train. No need to worry about me," said Ariana.

"Of course I'll worry," said Jacqueline, and she called her driver.

Luckily, Randy was still working in the area and suggested they take a cab and meet him at the Hilton Hotel. He had to would be there soon, and then he would drive Jacqueline and Ariana wherever they needed.

Jacqueline agreed, shoved her cell back inside her bag, and flagged a yellow cab. The pouring rain imposed itself on the city that night, and vacant taxis were no less scarce than they usually were on rainy nights. After a short wait, a cab pulled over and they jumped in.

"Where are we going?" asked Ariana.

"Let's go to the Hilton. Randy will be picking us up there."

Ariana smiled, cuddling next to her like a child through the short drive. Soon the taxi pulled into the circular driveway in front of the Hilton Hotel.

"Do you know what I want to drink?" asked Ariana as Jacqueline paid the cab fare.

Jacqueline rolled her eyes; after only two glasses of wine, she could feel a buzz. She wondered how Ariana could handle so much.

Ariana grabbed Jacqueline's hand and helped herself out of the cab. "Let's have a green apple martini!"

"None for me," said Jacqueline as they walked into the bar.

Jacqueline asked the bartender for sparkling water, and Ariana ordered her green apple martini. The place was unusually empty for a hotel bar. While they waited for Randy, Ariana told Jacqueline about her situation at work the past few months and her plans to come work in the city. She also mentioned that even though she had been successful in residential real estate in Queens, she felt ready to break into commercial deals or perhaps in-house residential sales in Manhattan—if she were fortunate enough to find someone who would hire her in the city, because those types of jobs were hard to come by. Ariana had a few connections with bankers and a friend who had just helped a developer get financing for a residential project near the Soho area. He had promised Ariana an introduction to one of the guys in charge of the sales team. Luckily, with her experience and personality, she could easily land the job.

Almost two hours had passed. Jacqueline worried about her sons being home alone, even knowing that her eldest son, Phil Junior, would call her if he woke up. He was fourteen years old and quite mature for his age. With that in mind, Jacqueline suggested that Ariana sleep over at her place, but Ariana refused, saying that she had an important introductory meeting with her banker friend at nine in the morning and didn't have a change of clothes.

Jacqueline asked for the tab before calling Randy, who still had not arrived. She stared at her screen in shock. It was past two in the morning.

"That's it, Ari. Let's go," she insisted.

"I have a job interview tomorrow. I can't stay over. I'll just grab a cab."

Right then, Jacqueline got a call from Randy. "Hello?"

"Hello, Mrs. Kingsley. Are you still at the Hilton? I just pulled up. I had to pick up a client who was stranded at the airport," Randy said apologetically.

Jacqueline was concerned about Ariana and glad Randy had finally arrived. He explained that his client had arranged transportation earlier that week, but Randy's partner had witnessed a traffic accident downtown and couldn't make it to the airport on time. Jacqueline calmed down the moment she sat in the luxurious SUV and helped herself to a small bottle of water. Randy always kept a couple on hand for clients, one of the few perks offered by the expensive driver services.

Jacqueline asked him to drop her off at her apartment, and he agreed to drive Ariana over to her short-term rental apartment in Queens, near where she used to live. There was no reason for Jacqueline to share any details about Ariana's current living situation, and Randy wouldn't dare ask—and didn't care to.

Randy pulled over in front of Jacqueline's building. A doorman approached the vehicle and opened the passenger door. Jacqueline hugged her friend good night, eager to step out.

"No way! Bastard!" Ariana cried, staring at the screen of her cell phone in disbelief. Embarrassed, Jacqueline shut the door abruptly, startling the doorman.

"Keep going, Randy," ordered Jacqueline. "What happened now, Ari?" she asked.

Ariana looked up, crying hysterically. "This can't be!" she cried as she leaned over to the driver's seat. "Randy, take me home to Forest Hills— you know, where I used to live."

"What happened?" Jacqueline asked.

Ariana showed her the text message on her cell phone. "Look!" she said, letting out a hysterical cry. "That son of a bitch! He's at my house right now. I'm sure he's in *my* bed with *my* husband! He can't even wait for me to sign the damn divorce papers!"

Ariana had received a text message from her neighbor about a blue car blocking access to the garbage cans. Jacqueline leaned forward. "Randy, let's go," she said, placing her arm around Ariana. "I can't let you go to your husband's house alone at this hour."

"That bastard!" said Ariana between sobs.

Randy drove without asking questions and glanced at them occasionally in the rearview mirror. He felt bad for Ariana. Jacqueline could only hug her and try to calm her down.

"How do you know someone is there? Maybe he's gone by now," said Jacqueline, and Ariana showed her the cell phone screen for the third time.

"Look! My neighbor sent me a text message!" Ariana screamed.

Jacqueline nodded in disbelief.

"See? I'm not crazy!" she said.

Jacqueline hugged her, hoping to help her cool off, but nothing she said or did changed Ariana's mood. Randy shook his head, and his gaze met Jacqueline's for a second in the rearview mirror. Their glances conveyed resignation, and without exchanging a word they realized that a night of drama with Ariana had begun. Jacqueline smiled feeling worn out, and he smiled at her and shrugged.

Chapter 2

The ride from Manhattan to Queens took longer than expected due to road construction near the Queensboro Bridge. Ariana cried uncontrollably, screaming and bashing her soon-to-be ex-husband. Jacqueline could only listen.

Randy had worked for the Kingsleys for many years. Before that, he had worked for Jacqueline's father and had known Jacqueline, as well as Ariana, since they were in their early twenties. Jacqueline and Ariana had been inseparable in college, and Randy had witnessed Ariana's drunken episodes more times than he cared to remember. He knew from experience that something bad was brewing for them that night.

After a while, Ariana calmed down some, though Jacqueline noticed her somewhat woebegone stare. Ariana prided herself on having an explosive temper, which she now combined with drunkenness, and Jacqueline was not optimistic about persuading her not to make a scene. Nevertheless, she insisted.

"Ariana, please. Let's forget all this nonsense. Please, stay at your place and be the bigger person—"

"I don't give a rat's ass about being the bigger person, Jacky! Do you have any idea how humiliating this is to me? You should be supporting me!"

"What do you hope to accomplish? It's past two in the morning, Ari."

"I have to face those bastards! Bet you they won't even look me in the eye!"

Carlos had ignored all of Ariana's texts and voice messages that week. His attitude only served to fuel her rage, and nothing Jacqueline said could help ease her pain. Ariana's divorce had come unexpectedly, and the changes had been the best excuse for her excessive drinking lately.

They finally arrived in Ariana's neighborhood. Randy had hardly parked the vehicle when Ariana jumped out of it like a madwoman and ran to the front of the house, fueled by her own fury. Jacqueline suddenly realized that bringing her here had been a big mistake. "Randy, I think we better get Ari back in the car. Look at her—she's out of control. I should've known better," said Jacqueline, staring out the window as Ariana kicked the front door of the house, seemingly oblivious that it was the wee hours of the night.

"Open the door, you bastards!" she screamed hysterically.

Randy turned to look Jacqueline in the eye from the driver's seat. "This is the worst I've ever seen her, ma'am."

Jacqueline agreed. "Oh, sweet Jesus," she said in a soft voice. "Please, Randy, go get her before they call the cops."

Randy stepped out of the vehicle and rushed to Ariana's side. He took her arm gently, but Ariana jerked out of his grasp, shouting and kicking the front door of the place she had once called home.

"Open the door, you shitface!"

"Ma'am, please. Let's get out of here," said Randy. "You and your husband can talk this over sometime tomorrow—"

"Are you taking his side?" demanded Ariana, staring at him defiantly. "To hell with the police!" she slurred, her eyes glazed over with drunkenness.

Jacqueline climbed out of the SUV and ran to Ariana's side. The next-door neighbors had just turned on the lights. Jacqueline was trembling with nerves.

"Let's go," she said, pulling Ariana's arm, but Ariana resisted. She looked possessed.

"I won't leave until these bastards tell me how long this has been going on!"

Someone had turned on the lights in the foyer. They all heard a quivering voice. "I would leave if I were you. We just called the cops!"

Johnny, Carlos's lover, was behind the front door. He had a restraining order against her, but as this was her house, he knew deep inside that he was breaking the restraining order, as well. He was peering through the long glass window at Ariana with wide, frightened eyes. Ariana made eye contact with him and broke free of Jacqueline's grasp, pushing her away like a wild horse.

Jacqueline stumbled and fell on the muddy lawn. Randy rushed to her aid. "Are you okay, Mrs. Kingsley?" he asked, extending his hand and helping her to her feet. Jacqueline nodded. Suddenly, they jolted in surprise, petrified by a horrific crashing sound. They turned, aghast, to see Ariana in Randy's SUV. She had crashed the vehicle into the house's front door.

"Oh, hell, no!" he lamented in desperation.

"Take that, you bastards!" shrilled Ariana with her head out the window. Jacqueline was shocked at her level of madness.

"This can't be happening," said Jacqueline. They heard police sirens approaching the chaotic scene.

Two patrol cars pulled into the driveway, blocking the crashed SUV. They spoke through the loudspeaker, advising Ariana to step out of the car. She refused. Again, they ordered her to step out of the vehicle, to no avail. The officers got out of their cars and ran to the SUV.

Jacqueline panicked when one of the cops pulled out his gun. "No!" she screamed, taking a few steps forward before she froze in fear.

"She's not armed!" Randy shouted.

Once more, the officers asked Ariana to step out of the vehicle, and this time she complied. The minute she stepped out, the two cops jumped on her like they would a deranged criminal and handcuffed her while she struggled, attempting to resist arrest. An ambulance had also arrived at the scene, and the police combined their efforts, helping the paramedics stuff her into a straitjacket before they took her away on a gurney.

Ariana's husband opened the door, now barely hanging from its hinges. "Who's the brilliant jackass that brought this drunken psycho to my house at three o'clock in the morning?" shouted Carlos.

Carlos was fit and taller than Randy. His bald head, thin lips, and big eyes didn't make him particularly attractive. These markedly peculiar features made him look like a cartoon character. Now, he stood outside the house in boxers and a gray hoodie, knee-high socks and flip-flops, caring little about his neighbors, who watched the scene and whispered among themselves. Carlos let go of the doorknob and threw himself onto the SUV, punching the hood of the vehicle, which was crumpled like a cheap tin accordion. He kicked the car, ranting and stomping around. Randy ran over and pushed him away. Jacqueline tried to explain to Carlos that Randy was not the one to blame for the situation, but Carlos wouldn't listen.

"It's your fault!" Carlos shouted, kicking the tires of Randy's SUV.

"Don't fucking kick my car! Asshole!" shouted Randy.

Both men were now in the spotlights of the police cars. "Hands up!" commanded an officer over the loudspeaker.

Carlos lunged at Randy, and soon they were mauling each other like two pissed-off teenagers. Randy managed to get away from Carlos, but the officers took them both into custody, forcing them into separate police cars.

Jacqueline stood immovable without articulating a word. She felt a painful knot in the pit of her stomach and thought for a moment she was about to faint. *This can't be happening,* she said to herself.

A female police officer approached her. "Excuse me, ma'am. Come with me," said the officer in a sharp tone.

"Am I under arrest?" asked Jacqueline.

"No, ma'am. We need you to sign a witness statement." The officer could see that Jacqueline was petrified and pale. Carlos's boyfriend, Johnny, ran from the scene. He got into his car and followed the patrol car to the police station.

Jacqueline filled out a form explaining how the situation had unfolded. She asked the officer for a lift back to the city, but the officer explained that she was not allowed to drive outside her jurisdiction. However, she was kind enough to drive Jacqueline to the nearest train station.

Jacqueline bought a one-ride card and rode the subway quietly. Daylight had arrived, and commuters were engaged in their early morning routines. Jacqueline looked around in a zombie-like state. The other subway passengers seemed to ignore her odd appearance and blank stares.

She got off the train, walked a few blocks, and stopped at the bagel shop. She was hoping the children were not awake yet. If they were, she planned to tell them she had stepped out earlier to buy them some breakfast. She made it to her building, entering nonchalantly through the golden double doors.

The doorman noticed her disheveled appearance. "Good morning, Mrs. Kingsley," he said. "Is everything all right?"

Jacqueline smiled, trying to broadcast the calmness she lacked. "Good morning, Tony. Yes, everything is fine," she said, walking straight to the elevator.

Jacqueline reached her apartment in a daze. Just when she opened the door, she realized the heel of her right shoe was missing. It had broken off when Ariana pushed her to the muddy lawn. "Oh, well," she said out loud and closed the door. The second she turned around, she stopped in shock at the sight of her husband, Phil. He was at the table with the kids, who were dressed and almost done with breakfast. She felt her blood pressure rise, then drop suddenly at the sight of yet another police officer, who stood tall next to her husband.

"You're home, finally," he said in a sarcastic tone.

"Good morning," said Jacqueline, looking at him pointedly before glancing at the children. They were neatly dressed in their uniforms, ready to go to school, and apparently surprised to see her come home the next day looking like a madwoman. She sensed that her eldest especially resented her absence from the home that morning.

Jacqueline kissed them like she would on any other morning, trying to convey normalcy, but nothing about her appearance or the circumstances was normal. Phil Junior could only stare at her tired appearance, smeared makeup, and messy hair. Her younger son, Mark, also gave her a look of uneasy puzzlement. Her disheveled looks diverted attention from anything she said. "Ariana had a horrible accident last night," said Jacqueline. "I had to go to Queens and take the train back to the city. Can you believe it?"

"Well," said Phil, "Mark called me at four in the morning and tried calling you too, but you were obviously engaged in more interesting endeavors."

"My phone died!" blurted Jacqueline, placing the paper bag filled with bagels on the table. "I can ask for a copy of the police report if you don't believe me. She had a horrible accident!"

"I don't need any report," said Phil on his way to the foyer. He grabbed his coat from the closet by the entrance and threw it on. He was immaculately dressed in a well-pressed suit. His wavy silver hair was slicked back, and he wore a hint of cologne with a fresh, clean scent.

"Let's go, boys. You're running late already," said Phil, assuming an air of superiority.

"I thought you were in Washington, DC!" said Jacqueline in a quivering voice. Phil ignored her and walked out with the boys.

She faced the officer with a forced smile. "I can explain, officer."

"Good morning, Mrs. Kingsley. I'm glad to see you're well," he said in a compassionate tone.

Jacqueline removed her mud-caked mink coat and left it on the floor as she sank down next to the officer, dejected. She had no idea what Phil might have said about her to the police officer. She glanced at him with a deepening hue of shame. "Officer, do you mind if I take a minute to change into something more comfortable?"

"Sure. There's no rush, ma'am," he replied.

"I'll be right back. I'll just take a minute," said Jacqueline and rushed to her bathroom. She showered and immediately felt better in comfortable, clean clothes. She pulled her hair into a ponytail, rushed back to the living room, and sat calmly. The cop listened to Jacqueline as she explained the incident at Ariana's house and told him that she had already filled out a report.

The officer stood briskly from the chair, placed his small notepad in his shirt pocket, and wished her a good day. He bumped into Donna as he stepped out of the apartment, and the maid glanced at him nervously.

"Oh! Good morning," said Donna, watching the officer walk out. "Jacqueline, is everything okay?"

Jacqueline shook her head. "Please, Donna, don't ask. I'm going to bed now. See that you take my mink coat to the cleaners. It's been quite a night," she said as she walked to her room.

Jacqueline lay in bed, thinking about her unsalvageable marriage, and knew that Phil would use this incident as the perfect excuse to fuel his constant escapades.

Phil didn't come home that day or night, and Jacqueline didn't expect him, either. Over the past year, Phil had spent more and more time at the office and would stay at their Hamptons home most weekends. Only a few times had he taken the boys with him, which was quite odd. He and the boys were very close.

Donna slept over that weekend at Jacqueline's request, and as a sign of gratitude, Jacqueline doubled her pay that week. Donna needed the money and was also pleased to help out with the children. She enjoyed them as if they were her own. She didn't have kids and had watched the Kingsley boys grow since they were toddlers.

That weekend, Donna took the children to a few birthday parties for their friends from school, and on Sunday afternoon they all went to the science museum, then capped it off with a fun evening at the movies. She had already taken them shopping for supplies for their school projects that Friday.

Jacqueline had lost her appetite and ate nothing but green tea and crackers throughout the weekend. By Tuesday night, Donna was worried and shared her concern, telling Jacqueline that she was starting to show the first signs of depression.

Jacqueline's marriage was in shambles, which was no secret to anyone who knew the couple well. Above all, Jacqueline counted herself lucky to have Donna, who would do everything in her power to help alleviate the tension in the house.

The Kingsleys had been very generous to Donna and her husband, who were humble, honest people and always expressed great respect and gratitude toward their patrons.

Jacqueline thought of Ariana and worried about her. She'd been trying to reach her ever since the altercation the previous Friday night, but all her calls went straight to voicemail. After a while, she figured that Ariana would reach out to her when she needed her.

Jacqueline had been consumed those past few days, doing everything possible to get her husband's attention, and couldn't understand why she was failing miserably. Phil was unpredictable, and in recent years he had shown the clear traits of a classic narcissist. His attitude toward those beneath his social status was shameful, even toward people more insufferable than he was. Since his fiftieth birthday, Phil had become obsessed with his appearance. He spent hours at the gym and at one of those terrible tanning salons that gave his skin an orange hue.

Phil hardly spent time at the house anymore, and the nights he did come home, the smell of tobacco and perfume lingered on his clothes. Jacqueline felt helpless, not knowing whether to keep quiet or demand his respect. When he came home with a familiar vanilla scent, Jacqueline had a hunch. This time her husband's love affair was a threat, she told herself.

Jacqueline had barely moved from the couch and was watching television on mute, absently sipping a cup of Green tea. The house lay in almost total darkness, the curtains closed. Donna was beginning to worry, and as her workday was coming to an end, she refreshed Jacqueline's tea pot.

"Would you like me to fix you something to eat before I go?" she asked.

Jacqueline smiled. "No, Donna. Thank you. Did you iron the boys' uniforms?.

"Yes, ma'am. Everything is ready," said Donna, putting on her wool coat.

"You can leave if you want; it's getting late."

Donna wished Jacqueline a good night and left her lying on the sofa, hugging the covers, with only the dim light of the television screen. Jacqueline grabbed her phone to call Ariana and saw an incoming text message.

"Good evening. I hope you're doing well. It was nice meeting you. Will."

How nice, she thought. Although she would have preferred a message from Phil.

Jacqueline waited a few minutes, unsure of whether to reply to the message, then smiled and texted him back: "Hi. Let me know when you're in the city. Maybe we could have lunch? J."

He didn't reply immediately, and Jacqueline wondered if she had been inappropriate for having suggested the outing. Perhaps she had been too forward, giving him the wrong idea. The screen blinked again.

"The other night you suggested dinner, and now lunch? How are things at home?" he wrote.

"Thank you for asking, but perhaps I could fill you in when we meet in person," she concluded.

William would be in the city to approve the purchase of some medical equipment the next day. The night they met, he had told her about his investment with new partners who were purchasing state-of-the-art equipment for their new facility. Jacqueline agreed to meet him the next day around five, at the same place where they had originally met. Just as she wrapped up her texting session with William, Ariana called.

Ariana told Jacqueline that the police had put her in a psychiatric ward for the weekend. On Monday morning, she had been released, thanks to the efforts of an attorney friend.

"You don't know what I've gone through!" said Ariana in a hysterical tone.

"I can only imagine," said Jacqueline. "Going out for drinks with you these days doesn't pay off, Ari."

"Oh, hush up, Jacky! All this drama is Carlos's fault."

"Yes, but he's not showing up at anyone's house crashing cars against the door at three in the morning," said Jacqueline.

"I have to go to court the day after tomorrow," said Ariana. "My lawyer friend is representing me."

"Well, hopefully he'll do a good job. God knows you need a hell of an attorney after that episode the other night," Jacqueline told her in a serious tone.

"But at least he won't be charging me for now. God knows I can't afford any more expenses these days," said Ariana.

"Get someone with experience, Ari. You can't afford to lose this case," said Jacqueline as she turned off the TV.

"An attorney isn't the only thing I can't afford. Can you believe I got fired from my job?"

"Actually, yes, especially if they know you got arrested and locked up in a psych ward."

"Let's meet tomorrow. I'll behave, I promise," said Ariana in a strained voice, and Jacqueline agreed to meet her. Ariana had no one and needed all the support she could get.

Jacqueline listened while Ariana complained about having to show up in court in just two days, and Jacqueline was amazed that her friend seemed so out of touch with reality, not realizing the magnitude of the problem she had brought upon herself with her out-of-control drinking.

Ariana mentioned that her attorney friend had suggested she take anger management classes, which she found offensive.

Jacqueline advised her to quit the bottle for a while and to get her life in order. Perhaps anger management wouldn't be such a bad idea after all. Ariana listened and disagreed. All she wanted now was to sell her house and wrap up her divorce, the sooner the better.

Jacqueline had thought about couples therapy and Ariana was dead against it. She insisted that, once lack of trust weaved itself into a relationship all hopes for its survival were completely lost.

"Marriage contracts should have an expiration date."

"That's not true, Ari. My parents were married for fifty-two years."

"You said it—your parents. In this day and age, marriage is a disaster. If we had to renew the marriage contract every five years, trust me . . . men would keep their asses in check!" Ariana said. "Sooner or later, they all cheat. Bastards . . ."

After a candid conversation, they wished each other goodnight and arranged to meet the next day. Jacqueline walked to her bedroom, then heard someone enter the apartment, slamming the door and jingling keys. She went to the foyer and saw Phil walking in. Until that moment, she had forgotten about his nasty demeanor and cheating ways.

"Hi, honey," she said calmly. "I'm glad to see you made it home tonight. I think we should talk."

He looked unnerved. He walked past her tongue-tied.

Phil was impeccably dressed as usual in a blue and white striped shirt and the white gold cufflinks with sapphires that Jacqueline had given him for Christmas years ago.

Jacqueline followed him to the bedroom, hoping he would agree to the idea of couples therapy. She had been thinking about it the entire weekend and was convinced that sessions with a professional would help restore their marriage.

"Are you okay?" she asked, caressing his arm.

Phil shoved her aside as he rushed into the walk-in closet and grabbed a brown suitcase that he laid flat on the bed, ready to pack.

Jacqueline watched him pull clothes from their hangers and toss them into the suitcase. She turned to him, aghast. "What does this mean?" she asked, numbly.

"Just what you see," he answered.

"Where did you leave the suitcase you took last week? Half your clothes are missing!" she asked with a look of puzzlement.

"Can't you see I'm getting all my stuff out of here?" he snarled as he carried on packing.

"Where are you running to now? To your twenty-something-year-old whore, right?"

"I can't stand you," he said. "Look at you! You're always fighting! I can't stand you anymore—"

"So now you can't stand me? You are successful thanks to me! You are who you are and have what you do because of me!"

"Not you—your father!" he said. For a fleeting moment, he felt ashamed. He knew she was right.

Phil Kingsley had a lot to be grateful to Jacqueline for, even when he wouldn't admit it. Unlike Jacqueline, Phil had grown up in one of the roughest areas in Brooklyn, raised by a single mother with scarce resources, and his childhood had been less than ideal. He had never known his father. In college, he had lost his mother to breast cancer and lost all the family he had when she died. Jacqueline's family had welcomed him with open arms despite their social differences, and Phil knew he owed much, if not everything, to Jacqueline and to her father.

Jacqueline wasted no time smashing his pride when she felt the urge to refresh his memory. "Thanks to me! I've given you my best years! I've given you all you have! A family! A career! And now that you have some sleazy twenty-something-year-old, gold-digging whore, you can't bear the sight of me?"

"Look at yourself!" said Phil. He glanced at her with contempt. "You are a mess, always screaming, clingy, and hysterical!"

"You're never here! What do you expect me to do? I'm always alone! What do you care if I'm bitter?" she sobbed uncontrollably.

"I don't want to be here, Jacqueline; we can't talk. You have no idea how to sustain a conversation. You just spend my money on ridiculously expensive junk. I can't take you to an office party without fearing you'll question any woman who works with me, like a damn Interpol agent! It's embarrassing and I'm sick of it!"

"What am I supposed to do? You have more time for them than me!" said Jacqueline, taking a stance in front of him. "You should tell me how best to deal with you and your sluts!

Phil glanced at her unaffected. "Jacqueline, we don't see eye to eye; we can't even talk, much less understand each other."

"What's your point?" she said. Phil threw the last few shirts he had snatched out of the closet into the suitcase. "I want a change," he said. "Please, Jacqueline, understand. Our marriage is over."

Jacqueline watched him close the suitcase, feeling his words like a stab to the heart. She wouldn't give up. Losing her husband to another woman was inconceivable to her. "We could go to couples therapy," she said quietly.

Phil shook his head as he placed the suitcase on the floor to roll it out of the room.

Jacqueline blocked his way. "So you'd rather go with your whores than work on your own marriage?" she screamed.

Phil pushed her aside. "At least they're entertaining," he said in a calm tone that only served to humiliate Jacqueline, who felt his words like a ruthless stab through the heart. How could the man she had loved all these years turn out to be such a tyrant?

The children, awakened by her screams, were now in her room. Mark stood by the door, pale as a ghost, with tears streaming down his face. "Mommy, why are you screaming?" he asked.

"It's nothing, honey. Mommy is just talking," said Jacqueline.

Phil approached the boys. "I'll pick you guys up after school tomorrow."

"Are you going on a trip, Dad?" asked Phil Junior in a low voice, staring at the suitcase.

"No. I told you, I'll be picking you boys up from school. We'll talk about this tomorrow. Now go to sleep."

The boys hugged Phil and kissed Jacqueline. "Good night, Mom," Mark said, and Jacqueline forced a smile and nodded, holding back tears.

Jacqueline's children were aware of the dysfunctional dynamics in their parents' marriage and had witnessed their fights rapidly escalating.

The boys had not yet left the room when Jacqueline grabbed Phil by the sleeve. "So . . . are you leaving me? You're leaving us for some kid who is young enough to be your daughter?"

"You're paranoid," Phil shouted. "You're crazy."

"Now I'm crazy?"

"My lawyer will contact you," he said.

Jacqueline felt her blood pressure rise like a bursting thermostat. She ran into the bathroom and grabbed a pair of scissors, then ran to their walk-in closet, blind with rage. "Do you want to leave?" she shouted. "Let me help you pack light, you asshole!"

Phil threw the suitcase down and ran to the closet after her. "What are you doing?" he shouted.

Jacqueline, possessed by pure madness, began to rip Phil's designer suits off the hangers, cutting them recklessly in half, then his ties and his shirts. Phil grabbed her arm, but she pushed him aside with such fury that he stumbled and fell against the wall. She was now stabbing his designer shoes with the scissors. Enraged, Phil grabbed her by the waist, dragged her out of the closet, and threw her on the bed.

"What the hell are you doing? Have you gone mad?" he shouted..

The children watched the chaos from the door, horrified.

"Why don't you stop fighting with Dad, Mommy? If you stopped fighting, Dad wouldn't leave," said her oldest son, Phil Junior.

Jacqueline regained her senses, still lacking a clear head. She sat on the foot of the bed and looked up, eyeing both boys with an exhausted gaze. "I'm sorry," she whispered.

Phil Junior and Mark both approached her, and Jacqueline hugged them, crying uncontrollably. A short while later, she calmed down and watched Phil grab his suitcase and walk toward the door.

Jacqueline looked his way. "Where are you going?" she asked.

"Far away from you," he shouted.

Silence reigned for a brief moment before being broken by the slamming of the front door. Phil had left, and Jacqueline felt for the first time in over twenty years that their relationship, as she knew it, was now over.

Chapter 3

The sun had not yet risen over the streets when the garbage trucks began their parade. Workers hung from the backs of the riotous vehicles, snatching garbage bags left on the sidewalk in front of the shops and restaurants.

The early morning light streamed through the gap between the curtains of Jacqueline's bedroom, waking her. She opened her eyes as the sunbeam warmed her face, then gasped in shock, realizing she had forgotten to set the alarm clock the night before. "The kids are late!" she shouted and jumped out of bed. She threw on her robe and rushed out of her bedroom to the kitchen. Surprisingly, the boys were there, alert and awake, in their pajamas and ready for breakfast.

The youngest, Mark, held a box of sugary cereal, and Jacqueline snatched it away. "No sugary stuff on school days," she said. "Go get ready, Mark. I'll make you guys some eggs."

"Yay! Are you having breakfast with us too, Mommy?" he asked excitedly. She rarely sat with them for breakfast on weekdays.

"Yes. Now go and get ready."

Phil Junior leaned over, kissing her warmly on the cheek. He was unusually tall for his age. "Do you still remember how to turn the stove on, Mom?" he asked in jest.

"Of course I remember, goofy boy," she said jokingly, and he smiled.

"When is Randy coming back, Mom?" he asked, shuffling his feet in the hallway on the way to his bedroom.

"I'm not sure," she said. "Don't you like the driver Dad sent for you yesterday?"

"He's too quiet."

"Well, good thing he doesn't need to talk; he only needs to drive, right?" said Jacqueline, carrying the dishes over to the breakfast table.

Jacqueline sat with her coffee, and shortly afterward the boys joined her at the table. Phil Junior looked surprisingly sharp in his uniform. Unlike him, little Mark was always intentionally casual, even in the sharply pressed blazer both boys wore as part of their stylish school uniforms. Phil Junior had his father's style. He was tall and always worried about the creases in his shirt, but his little brother was happiest in jeans, a T-shirt, and messy hair. Nevertheless, both children had impeccable manners, especially at the dining table. They kept their backs straight while seated, careful not to place their elbows on the table, and managed their silverware perfectly.

Jacqueline had done a good job raising her boys, and she was proud of them. She placed great importance on basic table manners and insisted that they read for at least half an hour before bedtime. Phil insisted that they express good manners with articulate speech, and at their young ages, they did just that without great effort.

Jacqueline served herself toast, cutting it into tiny pieces. She sipped her coffee as she swept the crumbs from one side of the plate to the other with her fork, not taking a single bite.

That morning, Jacqueline had awakened feeling melancholy. She had skipped dinner the night before but still didn't have an appetite. She was consumed by the quest for peace in her miserable marriage, and it was beginning to drain the life out of her. Though she worked hard to find ways to please her husband and make their daily interaction more bearable, his lack of compassion made her feel empty and hopeless.

Her constant ruminating made her seem absentminded, husband barely noticed her sadness. If he did, he didn't seem to care.

"Mom, when is Randy coming back to work?" he asked.

She smiled sympathetically but seemed withdrawn. "I don't know, sweetheart," said Jacqueline. "I haven't spoken to Randy since last week."

"Dad said Randy's accident was your fault and Ariana's. Is that true, Mom?" asked Phil Junior as he took the last bite.

"Did he say that?" Jacqueline asked.

"Yes!" said Mark. "He did. I heard him too." He nodded with big eyes. "He said you went out to have fun with Aunty Ari, and she got drunk and drove Randy's car and smashed it into a wall. Dad said you're like crazy people and Aunty Ari is a nut."

"Well, your father wasn't there," reprimanded Jacqueline, "and he didn't care to ask me about what happened, either."

"That's what Randy told Dad, Mom," said Phil Junior.

"These are grownup issues," said Jacqueline, changing the subject. She asked them about school and their upcoming projects.

Phil Junior was no longer on the honor roll, and Jacqueline had arranged with his teachers to find him a good tutor. His study habits were not as good as they had been over the past year, and Jacqueline attributed his lack of focus to his addictive habits with video games. She had warned him about his grades and the way he spent his spare time, telling him that if he didn't bring his grades up soon, she would forbid the video games and access to the computer altogether. Phil Junior was livid.

"Why, Mom? That's not fair!" he ranted.

She looked him directly in the eye. "What's not fair is for us to be paying a fortune for your school and have you bring home mediocre grades as if you were doing us a favor. There's no reason you should have a C average."

"But I only play games on the weekends!" Phil Junior complained.

"I'm not negotiating with you on this," Jacqueline insisted. "You either step up to the plate or say goodbye to your video games until the summer."

Phil Junior kept quiet, knowing he had no chance to win the argument. Mark had also done worse than expected at school. He told her how much he wanted to take horseback riding lessons, and Jacqueline was petrified. She knew that she would forever be wary of the idea. She had lost her younger brother, David, to a fatal fall while horseback riding, and even though the accident had happened over fifteen years ago, no one in the family had gotten over the loss. After David's death, Jacqueline's father had sold their beautiful country estate in Vermont and gotten rid of their three horses. Since then, none of the family members had dared consider riding lessons until now.

Mark had tried to convince her. He promised to work hard in school and improve his grades. Mark had always been playful in class. Phil Junior, on the other hand, was always well behaved, a brilliant student, and had brought home nothing but As until that semester.

Mark had been asking Jacqueline and Phil for horseback riding lessons for over two years now, but in the past Jacqueline had been completely against it. Now, she unexpectedly agreed on the condition that he improve his grades. The boy was beside himself and rose from his chair, throwing himself into her arms with a rush of excitement.

Jacqueline took the dirty dishes to the kitchen and suddenly heard someone opening the door. She peeked out, hoping to see her husband, but it was the maid, Donna, walking in with a broad smile.

"Good morning!" said Donna, full of energy as she hung her black wool coat in the closet by the entrance. "Leave the dishes there," she said to Jacqueline, who had begun to fill the dishwasher.

"Thanks, Donna," Jacqueline said. "Can you help me out with the boys? Phil hasn't called, and I have no idea who'll be driving them to school."

Donna nodded in agreement as they heard the house phone ring. Mark dropped his backpack and ran to answer the call. He talked for less than a minute, then hung up before Jacqueline had a chance to take the call.

"Who was it?" asked Jacqueline.

The boy ran back to the foyer, picking up his backpack from the floor. "Dad, Mom. He said he's downstairs," said Mark.

"Thank God! Donna, please take them down to the lobby."

Donna agreed. "Let's go, boys," she said.

The boys said their goodbyes and left to meet their father in the front lobby. Phil was already waiting by the concierge counter.

"Good morning, Mr. Kingsley," said Donna. He smiled halfheartedly.

Donna knew things were worse than usual at the Kingsley home. Nevertheless, she tried to portray the calm only a peaceful alliance could bring.

"Please, Donna, tell Jacky I'll be picking up the boys at school later today. I'll bring them back before their bedtime," he said.

Donna nodded and went back to the apartment to relay Phil's message. Jacqueline was making great efforts to clean up her closet after scanning the mess she had created the night before. Phil's suits and ties were ripped apart like old rags and spread all over the floor. How could she have allowed herself to go this far? Phil's infidelities had finally driven her to the brink of madness. The emotional abuse he subjected her to was unbearable, and she feared for her own sanity.

Phil and Jacqueline had had their share of quarrels over the years, but nothing like the night before. Phil's escapades had become commonplace, and nothing he did or said ever surprised her anymore. His absence from home had become more frequent and his cheating had grown worse over the years. Jacqueline preferred to turn a blind eye, to convince herself that all men cheated and Phil was no exception. All would be well if only she hung on and let him burn out that phase. However optimistic she tried to be, this mantra was shredding her self-esteem.

Phil would often make sarcastic remarks when Jacqueline felt comfortable enough to share her own opinions with him. He spared no chance to belittle her, and she was used to it now, walking on eggshells when he was around.

Phil had been the only man in Jacqueline's life, and until then, she had given him the power to dictate her mood and her own self-worth. She was dependent on his constant validation, and the lack of it made her even more obsessed with acquiring it. Their relationship was now a world away from how it had started twenty-five years ago.

Jacqueline and Phil had met at a cozy restaurant in Little Italy, a small neighborhood in downtown Manhattan. That night, Jacqueline's friends had organized a surprise dinner party in celebration of her twenty-second birthday. Phil was the only waiter on duty and worked a double shift that day. He was a tall, handsome young man, and very charming. He served them attentively throughout the evening and took care of all the arrangements, down to the last detail. Jacqueline's friends were quite impressed and enjoyed his presence as well as his sharp wit and sense of humor.

Jacqueline was not initially attracted to Phil, but he was very impressed with her. She was a young lady of refined manners, precarious and timid, which he found adorable. After the birthday party, Phil escorted the ladies to the taxi and wasted no time making his move. He handed Jacqueline a one-dollar bill with his name and number written in bright red marker, making his message impossible to miss. He told her he would appreciate it if she called him the next morning. He didn't want to impose, just to make sure they'd all gotten home safely.

Jacqueline smiled at his remark. At that moment, she felt the spark. No one had ever attempted to catch her attention in such a charming way. The ruse did not fully win her over, but it did get her attention. Jacqueline didn't hide her excitement and laughed as she shared the anecdote with her parents over breakfast the next morning. In those days, much as now, Phil had been a workaholic and worked day and night to pay off his student loans. During their courting days, he worked hard, and his only day off was dedicated to Jacqueline. In time she, too, fell deeply in love.

Jacqueline's father had been a successful and well-respected broker on Wall Street for many years. He groomed his future son-in-law for the same level of success. Phil absorbed all his advice like a sponge, and Jacqueline's father took him under his wing, covering all the expenses for his young protégé, including the courses and fees for the exams required to finally get his broker's license. Three years into their relationship, the young couple got engaged. By then, Jacqueline's dad had introduced Phil to the most powerful people in the business. Soon, the young Phil Kingsley became well known and admired for his work ethic, which helped him build a solid reputation in the world of finance.

Now, after twenty-four years of marriage, their lives were dull and different. They talked less every day, and Jacqueline attributed his evil ways to a middle-age crisis. Phil was a different man now, and Jacqueline shielded herself in denial, traveling in her mind to the beginning of their happy courting days. Those were the times she opted to remember.

Donna walked into Jacqueline's room, interrupting her line of thought. "Ma'am, what are those clothes?" asked Donna, staring at the pile of jackets, shirts, ties, and shoes.

"Old stuff. Just bring me a couple of garbage bags. Phil will figure out what to do with his rags," said Jacqueline, trying to hide the shame she felt for her outrageous behavior. She almost convinced herself that she had done the right thing by exploding in such a tantrum. Phil had humiliated her one too many times with his unrelenting love affairs. She had the right to retaliate.

Jacqueline helped Donna, and together they organized Jacqueline's closet. Donna cleaned the bathroom and changed the bedsheets before they went to the boys' rooms and thoroughly cleaned their closets as well.

Jacqueline sorted out the clothing that no longer fit the boys and was stunned at how fast they had grown. Most of the clothes she had bought for them five months before were too small.

Jacqueline picked up the T-shirts, vests, and trousers that no longer fit the boys. She stuffed them in garbage bags and told Donna to give them to children she might know who were in need of clothes. Donna, too, felt good about giving to those less fortunate and placed the bags by the foyer. She vacuumed the rooms, leaving the place spotless, while Jacqueline drew open the curtains in Mark's room and opened the window slightly, letting in a current of fresh air.

They were finished cleaning the apartment, and after a nice hot shower, Jacqueline lay down to rest. She awoke from her nap at the chirping of her cell phone and smiled as she glanced curiously at the screen.

"I'm in the city. Still up for a drink or coffee?" William had written. Jacqueline hesitated for a few minutes before replying. The day before, they had made arrangements to meet at the bar in the St. Regis hotel, where they had originally met.

A friendly outing would be a nice diversion from her troubles, and she planned to make it home before the kids were back from dinner with Phil.

She got ready quickly. She put on a little makeup and threw on some tight jeans with an oversized brown wool sweater and two long metallic pearl necklaces that completed her casual-chic style. She pulled her hair into a tall ponytail, put on some knee-high brown leather boots, and walked out of her room with her bag in her hand, ready to go. She had a unique sense of fashion and looked younger than her years.

As Jacqueline walked out the door, she got a call from Ariana and remembered she had made plans to see her the day before. She texted an apology, letting her know she would call her back shortly.

After a short walk, Jacqueline strolled into the St. Regis hotel bar and stopped in mid-stride. William was at the bar, talking to Ariana. "When did they ever meet?" Jacqueline said aloud, approaching them. Ariana was as loud as usual, joking as she normally would with any stranger.

Jacqueline tapped Ariana on the shoulder with an inquisitive look. "Well, well . . . so you two know each other?"

Ariana smiled. "Hello, darling!" she exclaimed as they hugged. "I called you a few minutes ago, but when I couldn't reach you, I figured I would come to the bar to kill a little time before I went over to harass your doorman," she said in an animated tone.

"Forgive me, Ari. I was going to call you when I got home. I forgot that I had plans to meet with William," Jacqueline said cheerfully and shook William's hand.

"I figured you would call back at some point," said Ariana, unconcerned.

William stood up from his barstool. "Come, sit here," he said. "It's a nice coincidence, if you ask me," he concluded. He seemed relaxed.

"I didn't know you knew each other," Jacqueline said, hanging her purse on a metal hook under the bar.

William smiled. "I didn't know her. We met just now, while I was waiting for you."

Jacqueline smiled at Ariana. "She's a lot of fun. I'm glad you met my best friend. Now I can spend time with you both and kill two birds with one stone!" she said jokingly. Deep inside, Jacqueline was worried that Ariana would get drunk like a college girl and cause a scene, similar to the last time they had seen each other.

Ariana never took anything seriously, and Jacqueline might just have to babysit her again.

They talked for a while, and when William spoke, Jacqueline and Ariana listened to him attentively, curious about his business endeavors, his separation arrangements from his wife, and the difficult dynamics that he now faced with his children. He only glossed over the subject, not wanting to give out many details. Jacqueline assumed that talking about such matters with strangers must be as embarrassing as it was painful.

William was a passive man and seemed generous and considerate. Ariana couldn't remember how it felt to date again and found her experience with William entertaining. Like Jacqueline, Ariana did not find him particularly handsome, but she was impressed by his proper demeanor. Her upbringing was a far cry from Jacqueline's, and, unlike her, Ariana couldn't tell the difference between forced propriety and the natural charm that the upper classes exuded effortlessly. There was a voluntary formality in his articulate speech, and Jacqueline could sense that, though educated, he most likely had humble beginnings. He lacked the spontaneous confidence of the well-bred from privileged backgrounds. Unlike Jacqueline, he had worked hard to get to where he was now.

Jacqueline accompanied Ariana to the restroom and warned her about her unrestrained drinking. The situation she had gotten herself into the last time was no joking matter, and Ariana agreed halfheartedly.

Ariana told Jacqueline that she found William interesting, and Jacqueline advised her to forget about the dating scene for now. Her focus should be on taking care of herself and her divorce. William could very well be a con man; they didn't know much, if anything, about him. For Ariana, any heterosexual man who could strike up a good conversation was enough to pique her interest.

Once they were back at the bar, William asked the waiter to move their food and drinks to another table. They sat on a sofa with a low table and a loveseat on the opposite side. It was more private, considering that the place was beginning to fill.

"Hope you don't mind that I asked to move over here," William said. "I'm sure you ladies will be more comfortable away from the crowded bar area. It's hard to hear anything," he said.

Ariana smiled in agreement as she stumbled against the corner of the loveseat. Jacqueline was quick to grab her arm, holding her up.

"I think we might want to get some water for Ariana," said Jacqueline.

"I only had three drinks."

"Yes," said William, "but mixing wine with liquor is never a good idea."

"It's no big deal," said Jacqueline kindly, smiling. "Let's get her some water and she'll be good as new," she said, trying to distract from a potentially embarrassing situation.

Ariana explained that the problem was not her drinking but mixing her drinking with her anti-anxiety medication. She had been taking Klonopin and antidepressants.

William stared at her, alarmed. "Are you taking Klonopin?" he asked. "It's very dangerous to mix Klonopin with alcohol."

"Whatever . . ." said Ariana.

"That can be a lethal combination," he said. "Surely you've read the side effects?"

Ariana rolled her eyes and sipped her water. "Don't worry, I'm only taking one milligram. That wouldn't hurt a fly," she said. Soon she was asleep on the sofa, curled into a fetal position.

William leaned toward Jacqueline. "Mixing benzos with alcohol is a bad idea," he whispered, sounding concerned.

Jacqueline shrugged. There was nothing she could do about Ariana's reckless ways. "I still haven't told you about what she made me go through the other night," she said. "Talk about drama . . ."

"What happened?" William asked, seemingly interested.

"I think I'd better not tell you, because you might think we're crazy," Jacqueline replied jokingly. She was not about to tell a stranger about the other night's reckless situation and changed the subject. Ariana was snoring like a chainsaw, and William could tell that Jacqueline was quite embarrassed.

"Don't worry," he said. "Few things surprise me nowadays."

"If I told you what she put me through the night I met you, you would be running for the hills," she said jokingly before letting out a small, spontaneous laugh. She actually meant it. Jacqueline patted Ariana's back affectionately. "Ariana and I have been friends since prep school. She's like a sister to me."

"Friends like that are hard to find," William said, and Jacqueline agreed, looking at Ariana. Her little nap was giving them a chance to chat amicably and get to know each other, if only a little. William told Jacqueline that he had been separated from his wife for seven months now, and Jacqueline asked him whether he thought his marriage was officially over or if he was really just separated while living under the same roof. "Some men claim to be separated, unbeknownst to their wives," she said.

He laughed at her sarcasm and assured her that they had been living separate lives for over two years and felt they needed to make their separate lives an official matter. He said it in a way that gave Jacqueline the impression he was trying to convince her. In all reality, she couldn't have cared less. Seeing him for the second time had made it clear to her that she was not at all attracted to him but instead found his company pleasant. There was a mysterious aura about him that was not easy to decipher at first sight.

William told Jacqueline that he and his wife were negotiating the divorce settlement before they brought lawyers into the mix, hoping to part ways on friendly terms. They had four children who were barely two years apart from each other. He managed to see them every other weekend. When Jacqueline asked him why he was getting a divorce, he avoided the subject, saying that his situation was complicated.

She perceived him as one of those people who wore their heart on their sleeve. She had a feeling that William had an ugly duckling complex. He was insecure, and it showed.

Jacqueline talked about her kids and vaguely glossed over her problems with Phil. William asked why she hadn't pressed for a divorce, and she said she didn't see that happening. They were not even separated, and she believed they would eventually work out their differences. Her children were too young, and she preferred to give them the stability that only two parents together under the same roof could bring. In reality, she wasn't sure she meant what she said. Phil was more hateful now than ever, and they barely spoke anymore. Jaqueline insisted on ignoring the fact that her husband had walked out on her a few nights before that night.

Jacqueline asked William about his wife's line of work, and he said she had quit working after having their first child. The truth was that Jacqueline preferred to listen to someone else's sorrows; she felt that knowing about another person's misery would make her troubles at home seem insignificant. Feeding that delusion made her optimistic.

"Did you have a good time?" William asked, curious about Jacqueline's remarks a while earlier.

Jacqueline forced a smile. "Oh my, very bad. I think that night caused the beginning of the end of my life as I know it," she confessed, feeling compelled to share something after listening to him share about the problems in his personal life.

"Why?" he asked.

Jacqueline shook her head in denial, urging him to change the subject, but William insisted. He leaned over. "But you looked lovely, very happy, when you left here," said William.

Jacqueline nodded.

"How many years have you been married?" William asked, sounding interested.

"Over twenty years," she said and drank some water. "The last ten years, I confess, have been hell. Something has to change, and if it doesn't soon, I just don't see a good ending."

"Have you considered therapy?" he asked.

"Yes, many times. But he refuses to go. "I see."

William told Jacqueline about his new business and mentioned that he didn't practice in his field at the moment. When she asked why he quit practicing, he said that he simply preferred the business aspect of it. All his licenses and continuing education were up to date, but he didn't expect to go back into practice anytime soon, if at all.

William and Jacqueline talked about their children's video game obsessions and agreed about the danger of such bad habits with technology. Their own childhood years had been different. Children had been happier when everything was simple, with less. Technology was taking over, annulling the warmth of human interaction, and kids interacted with each other like zombies these days. They both agreed that technology was replacing real, hands-on parent–child relationships.

Ariana woke up and smiled at Jacqueline. "What did I miss?" she said.

Jacqueline rubbed her shoulder fondly. "Are you okay?"

"Yes, of course. I think that martini got to me. Get me some water; I'm dehydrated," said Ariana, waving down the waiter.

Jacqueline grabbed her purse and pulled out her cell phone, taking a call from Donna.

"Hello?"

"Ma'am, you have to come home as soon as possible."

"What happened?" probed Jacqueline, rising from her seat.

"Please, ma'am, I don't know—"

"Are the children okay?" asked Jacqueline in a strained voice.

"They are not here, ma'am," said Donna in an urgent tone.

"I'll be right there," said Jacqueline and threw the cell phone in her bag.

"All good?" William asked.

Jacqueline closed her purse, hanging its chain over her shoulder. "I have no idea, but I need to go home," she said with a frightened stare.

Ariana grabbed Jacqueline's wine glass. "Don't worry, honey. I'll finish this one for you," she said. "Call me if you need me."

"Of course. I have to run," said Jacqueline. "Excuse me, William. Thanks for a nice time."

"I really hope all is well at home," William said, extending his hand, but Jacqueline rushed out, leaving the man with his hand out.

Jacqueline walked home with her face pale and nerves frayed. Her heart pounded violently as she approached her building, hoping that her kids were home safely. The rest of the world mattered little to her.

Chapter 4

Jacqueline hurried home as fast as she could, and the moment she set foot inside her building, she found a tall man holding a large envelope. He was seated on the red velvet couch next to a police officer.

"Jacqueline Kingsley?" he asked, and she nodded.

"You've been served," the man said, handing her a manila envelope without giving her any explanations, and he left.

She exchanged glances with the cop and, without giving much thought to the contents inside the envelope, ran straight to the elevators.

When she reached her floor, Jacqueline ran down the hallway and found her apartment door standing open. She walked into the foyer with a pale face and large eyes, dropping the envelope on the small coffee table next to the loveseat. A large brown suitcase sat at the end of the hallway. As she leaned forward to open it, she heard a noise from one of the boys' bedrooms.

"Donna?" she shouted as she walked with a determined stride, but Donna wasn't around. She burst into Mark's room and halted in surprise at the sight of Randy.

"What are you doing here?" she asked weakly.

"I'm sorry, ma'am," he said. "I'm only following Mr. Kingsley's orders." He continued packing the boy's clothes, tossing them into a black suitcase he had laid open on the bed minutes prior. Randy had also packed Phil Junior's clothes in the suitcase Jacqueline had bumped into moments ago at the end of the hallway.

"What do you mean?" asked Jacqueline with a puzzled look.

"Ask Donna; she was on the phone with Mr. Kingsley," Randy said.

"You could've told me you were coming over! Why are you packing the boys' clothes?" Jacqueline shouted in her usual nasal twang, her hands shaking with fear and outrage.

Randy kept quiet while packing the last few pieces of clothing. He wanted to take Jacqueline's side but felt obligated to Phil, who paid his salary and had helped him start his own chauffeur business. Jacqueline felt humiliated, as though the whole world was against her.

"Why are you packing Mark's clothes?" she insisted.

Randy closed the suitcase and carried it out of the bedroom. "I'm just following his orders," he said in a deep voice as he strode resolutely down the hallway.

"What orders?" screamed Jacqueline, losing her composure.

Donna entered the room, holding a document, and Jacqueline snatched it from her grasp.

"What's this?" she snapped. It was the papers from the manila envelope. Jacqueline had assumed they were divorce papers. She couldn't understand the chaos that Phil had created.

Jacqueline asked Donna what Phil had said. After a brief pause, Donna explained that Phil had sent a police officer to accompany Randy to the apartment in case Jacqueline tried to stop Randy from packing the boys' things. Donna had called Phil right away and convinced him not to send a cop upstairs. The presence of a police officer would add hostility to an already difficult situation. Phil agreed with Donna, and, though he didn't mention it, he was also concerned about what the neighbors would think. He had the police officer wait for Randy downstairs in the lobby.

Jacqueline glanced at the papers, feeling a knot of nerves in the pit of her stomach. She scanned the documents but realized her mind could not register one word at that moment. She looked up at Donna, who stared at her, as pale as a ghost and as stiff as a wire.

"Oh, ma'am," said Donna, "I think it's best to let Randy go. You can speak to Mr. Kingsley later, or tomorrow, and find out what's going on. Everything will be sorted out if we keep calm," she said.

"Phil is pushing his luck with me," Jacqueline said in a choked voice and ran after Randy, who was walking out of the apartment with the suitcases. She stood in the middle of the hallway near the elevators.

"Randy, please. What's going on?" she begged.

"Talk to Mr. Kingsley, ma'am," he said and stepped into the elevator.

Randy's attitude came as a disappointing surprise to Jacqueline, though she knew how intimidating Phil could be when he barked orders at his subordinates.

She retreated into the apartment and closed the door, then snatched the court papers from the table, holding her breath. Fear consumed her. She went through the documents cautiously, re-reading each line twice, and her firm demeanor transformed into a state of disbelief. *How is this possible?* she said to herself and felt a sudden loss of energy, and she collapsed into a chair.

Donna saw her from the kitchen and ran to her side.

"What's the matter, ma'am?" asked Donna urgently as she leaned over in complicity, holding Jacqueline's hand.

Jacqueline sat with a vacant stare, placing the document face down on the table.

Phil had taken out a restraining order against her. She was now being forced by the courts to have no contact with him or their kids for fourteen days.

Jacqueline covered her face with both hands, crying in rage.

"He wants to drive me crazy, Donna," she moaned.

"Who?" Donna asked.

"Phil!" Jacqueline screamed with the little strength she had left. "He's taken out a restraining order, Donna," she wailed between sobs. "I can't even talk to my own kids now!"

"Please, ma'am, please calm down. Everything will be okay," pleaded Donna. "Mr. Kingsley may have done this out of anger, ma'am. I'm sure that tomorrow he'll change his mind; he'll come to his senses. He can't do this."

The Kingsleys were at war now. Jacqueline never felt primed to deal with her husband's ruthless ways. His lack of compassion was nothing new to her, but after this stunt, she had no idea what to expect next. He had exhibited flawless cruelty. The time had come to start the battle; her marriage to Phil Kingsley was now over.

She had seen the impeccable example set by her parents, who had been married for over fifty years, and she felt guilt and overwhelming shame for the breakdown of her own marriage.

Jacqueline's parents had both passed away, and since she refused to reach out to her sister, she was completely on her own. Her sister, Jeanne, lived a world away in Geneva, Switzerland, and couldn't do much to support her anyway; she was also very egocentric, with a jealous streak she had aimed at Jacqueline while they were growing up. For twenty-three years, Jeanne's marriage had been as good as ever, and she had chosen not to have children. Jacqueline didn't have much in common with her.

Ariana and the housekeeper were the only ones Jacqueline trusted, and besides her children, they were all she had.

"Donna, please, can you stay over tonight? I think I'm going insane," Jacqueline petitioned in a calm tone.

"Yes, ma'am. I'll call my husband now," said Donna and left Jacqueline's side to get her cell phone from her purse, which she kept in the laundry room.

Unlike Phil Kingsley, Donna's husband was an unusually kind man with a positive outlook on life. Even problems couldn't disturb his inner peace. He was always happy, didn't care about social outings, and looked for ways to please his wife. He didn't feel he had much to say to anyone other than his few close friends, and he cared little about stirring up controversy at home. Donna called him at work that evening and explained the Kingsleys' troubles while he listened attentively. He encouraged her to stay with Jacqueline that night and give her much-needed support.

Jacqueline called her lawyer, Jeff, at his office, which was now closed. She tried reaching him on his cell phone, but he didn't answer. Now she suspected that Jeff would be on Phil's side and she would have to search for a new attorney.

"Why can't Phil just sit and talk like a normal person?" Jacqueline complained, throwing her cell phone on the bedside table. She lay in bed, staring at the ceiling. After much fruitless thinking, she called Ariana, but her calls went straight to voicemail.

Ariana was still at the St. Regis, enjoying William's company, and instead of calling William's cell phone, Jacqueline preferred to ignore them altogether and take a relaxing hot bath. Ariana hadn't thought of Jacqueline and was focused on making the best of her evening outing.

"A toast!" said Ariana in an animated tone. "To friends and friendship!"

William followed her lead with a boyish grin. He was almost embarrassed for her; she was beginning to sound incoherent. She glanced at him flirtatiously, and he moved from his chair, sitting on the couch next to her.

"So what's your story?" he asked, seemingly interested.

"What do you mean? I have many stories . . ." said Ariana, losing her composure.

"Married? Single?"

"Oh! That?" she said and seemed surprised at his question. "I'm soon to be a divorcee. Thank God for that! You wanna know what it's like to live without a sex life? Get married to a faggot!" she spat out with a hysterical cackle. William wasn't sure she meant it but found the remark almost repulsive. "Can you believe I never, ever had an affair" Ariana slurred, raking her short hair with her claw-like fingernails.

"No, I had no idea," he mused. "That must be disturbing." He raised his eyebrows, stunned. "Married to a gay man . . . that's a new one."

Ariana perceived William as somewhat monastic, and she liked that. There was something about controlling a man that she found empowering.

"And you?" Ariana said. "What's your story? When was the last time you had an affair?"

William smiled but didn't answer.

"Are you always this aloof?" she asked with a coquettish gesture.

"I'm usually reserved—most of the time," he said with a coy smile.

Now Ariana could tell his good boy facade was nothing but a shield. She was getting the impression he was not as elusive as he seemed.

Unlike Ariana, William was a light drinker. He drank some water, while she asked the waiter for one more drink.

They talked about their respective work experiences and pastimes. He mentioned that he didn't get much free time, at least not as much as he would have liked. William enjoyed sports, especially skiing, but since breaking his leg the previous winter, he had shied away from going back into it again. Since he'd begun working on his new business venture, he had little free time anyway; even a quick visit to the gym was rare.

Ariana was never too fond of the gym and told him so. She preferred to relax at the end of each day with a glass of red wine and, occasionally, a TV show. William watched little TV. He was not a fan of newscasts but did enjoy CNN. She asked him if he was a Democrat, and he looked amused.

"I don't talk politics," William said, and Ariana didn't goad him.

Ariana went on about her passion for the city and the real estate market. William also knew the market well, and Ariana was pleasantly impressed to converse with him. She chatted almost without breathing while William smiled and calmly listened. He sat by her side and looked as rigid as a concrete block.

Ariana reclined, resting her head on his shoulder trustingly as he pulled his cell phone from his jacket pocket and called Jacqueline. The call went straight to voicemail. Jacqueline had taken a hot bath to calm her nerves and was now fast asleep.

William turned his attention back to Ariana.

"What do we do now, Ariana? Do you need me to take you home? Or to your friend's house?"

She had fallen asleep. He summoned the waiter and asked for the check. The waiter nodded and rushed over to the bar. William was trying to wake Ariana, but there was no interrupting her dreams. He paid the tab.

The place was beginning to fill, and the manager approached William.

"Excuse me, sir," said the man in a low voice." Is she okay? Can I get you anything?" he said in an apologetic tone.

"I'm sorry, sir. The truth is, I just met her today," said William. "She did seem to have had a rough day."

"I understand," said the manager. William asked him to keep an eye on her while he retrieved his car. He would come back for Ariana in a few minutes and give her a ride home. The manager appreciated the gesture and offered to let Ariana know if she awoke in the meantime. The employees passed by the couch and served other customers, who glanced disapprovingly at Ariana.

A half hour later, the bar staff had begun to stare at her, still comatose and snoring. They exchanged questioning glances. The manager approached the bar and reached for the phone, ready to call security. Luckily, William was now rushing in through the entrance, and the manager exhaled, relieved.

"Hey, Ariana. I'll give you a ride home," said William, shaking her gently.

"Jacqueline?" said Ariana, feeling disoriented.

"Let's go. I'll drive you home. I tried calling Jacqueline a couple of times, but she didn't answer," replied William.

"It's okay. I'll take a cab home."

"I can drive you home if you don't feel well," he said as they walked outside.

Ariana was thankful for this well-intentioned gesture and accepted his offer. He had parked right next to the sidewalk in front of the main entrance.

Ariana climbed into the passenger seat. William closed the door and tipped the valet with a twenty-dollar bill for keeping an eye on the car while he ran inside.

As William drove out of the city, Ariana's silence was like a calming rose balm to him. The traffic crawled, but soon they were in front of the Queensboro bridge, and William turned on the GPS, asking Ariana for her address, but she didn't answer, and when he looked at her, her face was flattened against the window.

"Ariana!" he said, shaking her arm. "Ariana! Ariana! Wake up!" he urged, to no avail.

William pulled over to the side of the road, parked with the engine running, and hesitated for fifteen minutes before deciding to continue on his way home. She could always get a cab from there, he thought.

They arrived in his neighborhood, consisting of four tall buildings only a few feet from the Hudson River. On the ground floor of those four buildings, overlooking the river, were two restaurants and an ice cream parlor next to a small shop.

William followed a curved driveway into an underground parking lot and turned off the engine. Ariana jolted awake the second he got out of the car and slammed the door.

"Where am I?"

"We're in the parking lot of my apartment building," he said, extending his hand to help her out of the car.

"I'm not going anywhere! Are you crazy? Where is this place?"

"New Jersey, but don't worry. We're not far from the city. I can pay for a cab. Look," William said, "I tried to wake you to ask for your address, but you were so sound asleep that even a passing train couldn't rouse you. If you want, I can call a taxi to take you home"

"Why did you bring me to New Jersey? You're shameless! I was brought here against my will! I could report you for kidnapping," Ariana said, trying to buckle her seat belt again. "Take me to the hotel; I'll stay with Jacqueline," she argued.

William was a reserved man who avoided confrontation. He nodded in assent.

This is incredible, he grumbled to himself as he got into the car. He started the engine and screeched out of the parking lot. "Really?" asked William indignantly.

"Seriously, what?" muttered Ariana.

"Would you really accuse me of kidnapping?"

"If this isn't kidnapping, then what word would you use to define taking a person from one place to another against their will?" Ariana demanded.

"What will?" William said, raising his voice. "An hour ago, you had the will of a dead fish! You should be grateful I tried to help you. I don't even know your last name!"

"You men find excuses for everything," she retorted, looking out the window.

"I'm not that kind of person. Clearly, you don't know me."

The ride from New Jersey to Manhattan was over fairly quickly. William didn't care to strike up a conversation with Ariana, and when she asked him to drop her off at the nearest train station, he refused. He preferred to return her to the same place where they had met only hours prior. After Ariana's threat, he had decided not to take any chances.

Back in the city and only a block from the St. Regis hotel, William parked the car. They walked back to the hotel lobby, and Ariana looked lucid and alert. She realized she had been unfair to him and felt horribly rude.

"I have an idea—let's start over!" said Ariana playfully.

William smiled as the tension between them dissipated unexpectedly. "What are you suggesting?" he asked.

"What's your favorite drink?"

"Scotch, on the rocks. But I have to go. I'll take a rain check on that drink," he said, turning to leave.

"No! I'm inviting you to have a scotch with me! I know I've been a little rude," admitted Ariana.

"Yes, but it's fine with me. You should know I don't get offended easily," William said jokingly.

Ariana insisted on having a drink and held on to his blazer, making it impossible for him to leave. She finally won him over, dragging him with her to the now half-empty corner of the bar at the St. Regis.

William had finally succumbed to Ariana's charms and was flattered by her attention.

"Okay," he said. "Come on!"

Ariana followed him. "I promise I'll call Jacqueline to come get me. I'll stay with her tonight."

"Okay, but call her now," He insisted.

Ariana left the bar with her cell phone in hand and returned a couple of minutes later. William ordered a glass of water, and she ordered her apple martini and a scotch on the rocks.

"What did your friend say? Is she coming?" asked William.

"Sure!" she said. "I just sent her a message. She'll be here shortly. No worries."

As they talked, Ariana bombarded him with questions, some personal and others not so personal. He responded to them courteously without revealing many details. She was beginning to face the awkwardness of the single life and couldn't seem to adjust. He told her that he had been married most of his adult life and when women came on to him at the gym and at work, he found them awfully shallow. Ariana listened without judgment. She couldn't believe that a decent-looking guy like him, with an above-average career like his, could escape the piercing eye of a single, sexy alpha female. She had no doubt there was more to his story.

After several hours passed without a trace of Jacqueline, William suspected that Ariana had never called her friend and rose from the barstool. "I'm calling a taxi for you. I have to go, but I don't feel comfortable leaving you here alone," he said, pulling out his wallet and paying the tab.

Ariana drained the last drop from her glass and grabbed his arm. "It wouldn't be a bad idea if I stayed here tonight," she hinted.

William was exhausted and eager to call it a night but found it only proper to walk Ariana to the reception area.

"Here, give them my card," she said. "I wouldn't mind if you walked me to my room—wouldn't want to get lost. This seems like a big place."

William smiled, shaking his head. "You won't get lost. You're a grown woman. Trust me, you'll be just fine."

Ariana giggled at his remark.

The receptionist greeted them cordially. "You're in luck," she said. "We have a room. The Astor Suite—do you want it?"

"Yes, whatever, but let's wrap it up quickly. I'm dead tired," said Ariana. "William, bring me the form to sign whenever it's ready. I'll be over there," she said, pointing at a loveseat only a few feet away.

The receptionist made a few attempts to charge the room on Ariana's credit card. She glanced at William, who was stiff, watching her with a drawn face.

"Excuse me, sir," said the receptionist. "Both her credit cards were declined. Do you have another one?"

"Hmm . . . wait a second," William said and approached Ariana. "Hey, Ariana, your cards are not going through. Do you have another one? Ariana?" He crouched in front of her and found that she had fallen asleep again.

William walked back to the desk. He seemed exasperated, and the counter manager, who stood by the reception desk, had taken notice.

"Is everything okay?" asked the tall man with pale skin and a fleshy face. William sighed in frustration, his palms sweaty from nerves.

"Okay, how much is it?" he asked, pulling out his wallet.

"Let's see . . ."

William eyed Ariana over his shoulder, hoping to see her awake, but she seemed to be engaged in conversation, in the middle of a dream.

"Two hundred forty-five dollars, with tax," William heard the reception manager finally said.

"Okay, I'll take it," said William reluctantly, taking out his American Express card.

"Very well," the manager said. "I need your identification."

William completed the paperwork and had the keys to the beautiful suite in hand when he approached Ariana. He hoped she would awaken long enough to make it to the room, but that was too much to ask. She was unresponsive, and the counter manager approached them.

"Excuse me, sir. We have a wheelchair here in the back—"

"I think that might be my only option at this point," said William in resignation.

"I'll be right back."

The manager showed up minutes later with the wheelchair the hotel staff used for occasional emergencies. William nodded gratefully as he lifted Ariana by her arms and placed her gently in the wheelchair. The manager guided them to the service elevator, and in a few minutes, they arrived at the suite. The manager said goodbye and wished them a good night. William walked over to the door, grateful for his kindness, and gave him a tip.

"You can keep the wheelchair until morning," said the hotel manager. "Someone will come pick it up then," he added and left.

William surveyed the room, his face haggard with worry. What now? he thought.

The suite was medium-sized with a small living space. It had a sleeper sofa, a television set only in the sitting area, and a large desk facing a window with a view of the street.

William rolled the wheelchair to the edge of the bed, and as he lifted her voluptuous body effortlessly, Ariana awoke and their eyes met. William simply smiled, and suddenly she grabbed his tie, pulling him toward her aggressively. They fell together onto the downy bedding, and within seconds, she pounced wildly on top of him, certain that after a steamy night of passion, he would not complain.

Chapter 5

Jeff returned Jacqueline's call the next morning and listened attentively while she vented. He was indignant when he heard that Phil had taken out a restraining order against her and admitted that he wasn't at all surprised. Jeff was not close to Phil and the two had not spoken for months. Jacqueline was profoundly relieved that Phil had made no attempts to contact Jeff for representation in their divorce case.

Jeff told her that he had lost respect for Phil nearly six months prior when Phil invited Jeff for drinks. That night, Jeff saw a different side of Phil Kingsley and was disappointed by his condescending demeanor toward the bartenders. His compulsive drinking had spiraled so far out of control that he could barely walk when they left the place. His friend's driver made it his business to give him a lift, ensuring he arrived home safely. Jeff didn't much care for Phil's friends, either. They seemed like greedy banking crows, and since that night, Jeff had chosen to keep his distance from Phil. They had little in common, and unlike Phil, Jeff led a clean life and a much healthier lifestyle.

Jacqueline told Jeff about her psychotic moment the night before, describing how she had cut Phil's clothes to useless shreds. After conjuring an improvised laugh, Jeff asked her if she had ever undergone a psychiatric evaluation, and she responded that she hadn't.

He knew Jacqueline well enough to recognize her reckless act as out of character. She had always been the moral compass of the group during their younger years and he knew that she wasn't fond of drinking excessively, even on special occasions.

Jeff was blunt: If she stayed with Phil and continued to deal with his manipulative ways, she could end up losing her mind. She agreed. Gaslighting and mental abuse could push any woman to the brink of madness, causing her to question her own sanity and self-worth.

Jeff had been a good friend to Jacqueline throughout the years, and she trusted his professional opinion implicitly. After all, he was among the best family attorneys in the city and knew from experience the kinds of stunts men pulled before filing for divorce. He told Jacqueline he had a hunch that Phil was setting up the perfect scenario, building a case against her to seize custody of the children.

When Jacqueline expressed doubt about his suspicions, Jeff recounted the story of his last client, whose husband was a well-known chiropractor in Manhattan. The man had gone as far as arranging for his partners to demote him from his CEO position in the company for an entire year, enabling him to prove a reduction in salary to the court so he wouldn't have to pay as much alimony. He had placed all of his assets in a different corporation, in someone else's name. Of course, his efforts were futile—Jeff's first-class investigative team uncovered his elaborate fraud by showing the judge clear evidence of his facade. The man had no choice but to acquiesce to his wife's fair request plus a generous alimony schedule. Jeff and his team had won the case with flying colors.

Jeff was eager to help Jacqueline, having seen firsthand the kindness in her heart. He was deeply sorry for the pain she had endured while dealing with Phil and his ruthless ways. Phil took all he wanted with no consideration for the woman who had borne him two children, and Jeff knew it.

Jeff and Jacqueline agreed to meet in front of the downtown courthouse within an hour. Jacqueline hung up the phone and began her day, preparing for battle, while Jeff called his secretary to cancel his appointments that morning. Luckily, he had nothing of import scheduled that day.

Jacqueline left the house elegantly dressed, but without a hint of makeup except for some lipstick. She hid her emaciated appearance behind black Versace sunglasses that were large and round enough to cover half her face. The flamboyant accessory had little to do with the weather or the occasion.

Traffic was in the thick of rush hour, and finding a vacant taxi was a mission in itself for anyone in Midtown that morning. After waiting a short while, Jacqueline got into a cab and soon arrived downtown. She stepped out of the yellow cab onto the street facing the courthouse and opened her umbrella against the rain that had just begun to bombard the streets. Jeff was nowhere in sight. Her stomach churned; he was always punctual. Had he undergone a change of heart? The thought overwhelmed her with discomforting paranoia. Suddenly, she heard someone calling her name and turned, exhaling in relief at the sight of Jeff crossing the street. He waved from the other side of the pavement, and she smiled.

Jeff was well dressed in a suit and a black coat that fluttered in the wind as he rushed through the intersection. He seemed approachable but sophisticated in a red scarf with a brown leather briefcase that gave him a formal rather than authoritative bearing. Jacqueline calmed. Her rescuer had arrived.

"Good morning, Jacqueline," he said sympathetically, squeezing her shoulders.

"Good morning, Jeff. I apologize for messing up your schedule. I never thought Phil would go to these extremes."

Jeff smiled, patting her back as they climbed the stairs to the imposing building. "Don't worry," he said. "Everything will work out just fine. Relax."

Jeffrey Hurst's tall, athletic build, piercing blue eyes, and full head of dirty blond hair impressed anyone who caught sight of him. He was assertive but not intimidating due to his disarming smile. There was nothing cocky about him. His captivating charisma was bright enough to charm snakes.

Jeff was the optimistic type, a rather unusual quality for an attorney who negotiated divorces. He found humor in the worst scenarios, which could always make his clients feel at ease. His sense of humor and hopeful outlook served to calm the worst of moods while helping his clients realize that things could always be worse. Even when Jeff sensed that events might not go as planned, he emphasized the positive before breaking the bad news to his clients. He was an animated and dedicated lawyer who, for the most part, argued effectively and persuasively at court hearings.

"Let's see how we can fix this disaster that's driving you insane," Jeff said. "I wonder what's behind Phil's crazy moves." He hugged her again, like a comrade who had put in a long day of work at her side.

He knew just how to cheer her up, and when she admitted she had questioned her own sanity over the last few days, he chuckled. The smartest people in history were usually perceived as having some insane streak by ordinary mortals, he said, and Jacqueline laughed at his remark.

She took his arm as they walked past the security in the building, and Jeff explained that he had taken the initiative that morning by calling the judge to ask for an emergency hearing, which was granted without a hitch.

Jeff had contacted Phil and his lawyer, Brandon Slayer, who was almost as good an attorney as Jeff. They had been classmates at Yale Law. When Jeff called him on the way to court, Slayer mentioned that Phil claimed Jacqueline had lost her mind and he wanted a divorce. Slayer warned Jeff that Jacqueline should take the settlement Phil was about to offer. If Jacqueline objected to his conditions, Phil threatened to take full custody of the children and force her to submit to a psychiatric evaluation.

Jeff told Jacqueline about the threats, and she laughed. "He's an imbecile!" she snorted. "I haven't seen a psychiatrist or psychologist, ever! Phil can't make me go through an involuntary evaluation, can he?"

Jeff shrugged his shoulders, his face drawn. "I don't know the real story, Jacky. But when I spoke with Brandon, Phil's lawyer, he told me Phil sent him some pictures."

"Pictures of what?" Jacqueline challenged. "I've never taken any compromising pictures!"

"Jacqueline," Jeff intimated, stepping closer and lowering his voice, "in the pictures, you were in your husband's closet with a pair of scissors, stabbing holes in his shoes." Phil's attorney hadn't given him further details—except that if Jacqueline didn't want to face a divorce war, she'd have to resign herself to whatever Phil offered without complaint.

"What *he* offers? He's the one who's been cheating on me for years! I'll keep custody of my children and take half of what we own. Period!" Jacqueline proclaimed.

"I'll get the rest of the story when I talk to the judge, but remember, on the basis of those photos, the judge may very well require you to go through a court-ordered psychiatric evaluation. The process can take months, or even years. Your boys will be affected by it."

Jacqueline froze for a moment, then broke the silence with watery eyes. "Good God! It's my fault, Jeff," she said apologetically.

"I don't think you have much in your favor, Jacky," Jeff said, sounding concerned. "Given the evidence, it would be easy for the judge to assume you're emotionally unstable. We have to counteract the effect that Phil's allegations might have. It's up to you to come up with a story that makes you the victim in this case."

Jacqueline sat on a bench in the middle of the hallway while they waited to see the judge. Only a few minutes had passed when Jeff broke the silence. "Phil seems reluctant to negotiate." He exhaled slowly, exhausted at the thought of Phil's irrational tantrums.

"I can't believe he took pictures of the closet," Jacqueline admitted, thoughts of that crazy night spinning in her head. "I have no idea how or when he could've taken them."

"Why did you lose control, Jacky?" he asked, placing his hand on her shoulder reassuringly.

"I don't know, Jeff. I don't know."

"We all know that Phil has never been a saint, but losing your cool like that?"

"I think he just wants to drive me crazy," said Jacqueline in a quavering voice.

"Knowing Phil, I think he wants to take this case all the way."

"Do you think he'll try to take the kids? I swear I'll die . . ."

Jeff calmly confirmed her fears. "You know I wouldn't lie to you. He's already trying, Jacky."

She nodded absently. Jacqueline thought of Ariana and her rampage, the night she had crashed Randy's SUV into her husband's house. Ariana had blamed her recklessness on a drunken stupor, and while she was not a self-proclaimed alcoholic, the story had served as the perfect excuse to shorten her stay in the psych ward and keep her out of jail. Jacqueline sat straight-faced and leaned closer to Jeff.

"I was drunk," she confessed in a low voice. Jeff turned his gaze in disbelief.

"You? Drunk?"

"Yes. Phil knew I had been drinking that night," she said. "He knows I can't handle alcohol. I rarely drink."

Jeff stared at her, trying to read the truth in her eyes, analyzing the situation and the case. It was the only excuse that could be viewed favorably under the circumstances.

"All right, Jacky. What happened that night?" he asked in a scolding tone.

"I asked Phil about his absence at home. The kids always wanted to know why he never had dinner at home anymore, and he finally admitted that he's dating some girl from the office."

"How long has this been going on?"

"Over a year . . . What was I supposed to do?"

"Why didn't you tell me about that this morning? Don't you think I should know?"

"I couldn't think straight. How do you expect me to remember every detail?"

"Okay, then how did you progress from arguing with Phil to cutting up his clothes and stabbing his shoes with a pair of scissors? I'm just asking. The judge might just want to know," he said.

"He pushed me when I told him to stop seeing her; that's when I went nuts!"

"I guess that's what we'll tell the judge—"

Jacqueline nodded. "You know I was drunk! He got me drunk on purpose!"

Jeff scrutinized her expression. "Alright, then," he said. "We'll say that Phil knew you were drunk and he provoked you to the point of madness."

Jacqueline nodded.

"Where were the children?" Jeff asked.

"Sleeping. They didn't see anything until later, when they came into the room and Phil was already holding his suitcase, ready to leave," she said.

"Is there anything else I need to know, Jacky?"

She shook her head.

Shortly thereafter, an officer approached and guided them straight into Judge Marshall's office.

Jeff spoke for Jacqueline, and she sat watching the two men without saying a word.

Meanwhile, in the suite of the St. Regis hotel, Ariana was just waking up. She opened her eyes and lifted the covers to find herself naked. She had no recollection of what had happened with William at the bar the night before. The sliding door that connected the bedroom to the small living room of the suite opened, and she pulled the sheets up to her neck. William entered the room, and she smiled.

"Good morning," he said, sitting on the edge of the bed.

"Good morning to you. It's a pity I can't remember anything."

William laughed. He was dressed in the same suit he'd worn the night before and had not yet put on his tie or jacket.

"Why don't you refresh my memory?" she hinted with a suggestive smile.

"I would like to, but I have things to do."

"Typical!" she screamed, watching him exit the bedroom. She rose from the bed with the sheets tangled around her like a Greek muse. "Hello?" she shouted.

"I have meetings to attend, and I already had to cancel a conference call this morning," he said. "Don't get me wrong, you're a lovely lady."

"You're not too bad either," she replied proudly. "Actually, it's all good. If you were so spectacular in bed, surely I'd have some recollection of it," she said, stepping into the shower.

William pretended not to hear her passive-aggressive response as he walked to the door.

"I'm going downstairs to check out now. If you don't have any cash, I can lend you some in case you need to grab a cab."

"What do you take me for? I'm not some homeless tramp!" said Ariana petulantly, stepping out of the shower.

"Do you not remember that your credit cards were declined?" asked William as he watched Ariana put on the white hotel bathrobe and wrap a white towel around her hair. "Don't you remember?" he insisted, holding the door open.

"I'm sure Carlos had everything to do with it. He's so stingy." She walked to the living room table and poured herself a cup of coffee.

William had ordered room service, and the tray was still on the living room table with some rolls and two silver thermoses of coffee and milk.

"I must advise you not to drink while taking meds. It's very dangerous," said William and left the room.

"Thank you!" she drawled sarcastically. Minutes later, she was dressed and freshened up, making herself presentable with the few cosmetics she had in her purse.

William arrived at the reception desk with the checkout summary the staff had slipped under the door that same morning.

"Can I help you, sir?" asked the young receptionist.

William shook his head. "This is wrong," he said, handing the bill over to the receptionist.

She examined the paper. "The charges are correct, sir."

"This is not the rate they offered me last night."

The young woman excused herself and returned minutes later with the shift manager. "Good morning," said the man. "Judith tells me you have doubts about the charges."

"Yes. Last night they offered me the Astor Suite for two hundred and forty-something dollars, but here you're charging me one thousand three hundred and eighty-five dollars!"

"Impossible, sir. We don't offer the Astor Suite for two hundred dollars. Actually, there are no rooms in this hotel for that rate, Mr. Harron."

In reality, he had perceived it as unusually inexpensive when he first heard the price but figured it would be indelicate to complain.

"Here, use this card," he said. A moment later, as he was signing the credit card slip, he saw Ariana. She appeared agitated as she ran toward him from the elevator, carrying his jacket and tie.

"Here!" she said, thrusting his tie and jacket into his hands.

"Are you okay?"

"No!" she answered, staring blankly, panting, and clutching his arm. "I'll never bother you again, but you have to take me to Queens now."

"Where?" asked William. He rolled his tie into a bun and tucked it neatly inside his pocket before putting his jacket on.

"I have a court appointment at eleven thirty, and it's almost eleven!"

"Look, lady . . . I already canceled my appointments this morning for you. Go get a cab," he countered, taking out his wallet.

"No! You have to give me a ride to court! You made me stay here, so now you have to take me to the courthouse!" Ariana insisted.

"Grab a cab."

"I can't waste time looking for a taxi," she screeched. "Most of those yellow cabs don't cross into Queens. If I don't show up on time, they can hold me in contempt. Please! I promise I won't bother you after this last favor."

"Fine," he said. "But then it's goodbye and good luck, all right?"

"Yes, yes! Thank you," said Ariana, and she called her lawyer. The lawyer helped calm her down and informed her that she'd need to talk to the officer assigned to her case before she saw the judge. There were a few cases ahead of hers, and based on the speed things were unfolding at court that morning, she had little to worry about as long as she made it before noon. In less than an hour, William pulled up to the courthouse.

"You can leave me over there," Ariana said. William drove along the sidewalk and stopped the vehicle near the entrance.

Ariana thanked him and kissed him on the cheek. She slammed the door and trotted up the stairs to the building.

William was relieved to see her go, hoping never to run into her again. The second he stepped on the accelerator, he found that he could barely turn the steering wheel. He got out of the car, fearing the worst. "Shit!" he shouted, livid. One of the front tires of his shiny vehicle was completely flat.

After rummaging through the trunk of his car, he remembered loaning his tire iron to a colleague who hadn't returned it. Closing the trunk with a sigh, he saw a janitor sweeping the sidewalk in front of the courthouse. "Excuse me," he said, "I have a flat tire but no tools to change it. Could you give me a hand?"

The old man removed his headphones and admired the shiny black car. "Yes, of course! I'm sure Tony at the grocery store can help you," he said, gesturing toward a small convenience store. "He's over there."

William could see the sign about two blocks away. "Tony, is it?" he asked.

"Yeah. Tony is the owner. I'll be here for a while. Tell him I sent you, and I'll keep an eye on your car," said the old man.

William rushed over to the grocery store. He walked in, sniffing the peculiar odor combination of fried tortillas and coffee.

He approached the counter. "Good morning," he said, leaning on the counter, as a short man emerged from the bathroom.

"What's up?" the man asked, wiping his hands on a paper towel.

"Are you Tony?"

"Yes, and you?" said the man, frowning.

"I was dropping someone off . . . and, well, I have a flat tire. I don't have a tire iron. The man who sweeps the sidewalk told me you could help me."

"Where is your car?"

William turned and pointed to the judicial building. "Over there."

"Wait. I'll go with you," Tony said as he shambled to a little room next to the refrigerators. He grabbed a black vinyl sack. "Lenny! Lenny!" he shouted.

"What? I'm taking inventory!" a woman hollered from the back of the shop.

"Come up to the register! I gotta step out a sec to change a flat tire!"

"This is a grocery store, not a car shop!" declared the heavy-set woman, limping to the side of the counter.

William and Tony left the store and crossed the street toward the court building. William looked around, but his vehicle was nowhere in sight.

"Where is your car?" Tony asked.

"I left it right here!" said William. But the car was not there, and neither was the old man. "My car was here . . ." he said again, bewildered.

"Today is not your lucky day, man," Tony said, pointing to a sign in front of the stairs that read, "Tow Zone."

"This can't be," William said, shaking his head. "I was only gone for a few minutes!"

Tony patted William on the back. "I had my car towed three times in one week!" he said, holding the black vinyl bag. "These people seem to come in spaceships instead of trucks. I don't drive to work anymore. The train is better for me." He headed back to the store.

"Where's the impound lot?" William shouted to Tony, who was already half a block away.

"It's not far, about twenty minutes," he answered, leaving William on a bench by the stairs. William was about to call a transportation company when he heard a shrill voice approaching. He turned to see Ariana, who had finished with the judge in record time and was now strutting confidently down the courthouse stairs with her lawyer.

"Hello, William! You're still here, waiting for me? What a doll!" she said flatly.

"No. My car was towed," he grumbled, rising from the bench. Ariana introduced him to her lawyer, who confirmed that the impound lot was a twenty-minute drive away and offered William a ride. William thanked him as he followed along to the parking lot.

"And I thought I would never see you again . . ." said Ariana jokingly.

William was not superstitious but was beginning to suspect that his initial encounter with Ariana had brought him horrible luck.

The lawyer's car was a tiny two-door Mazda that resembled a toy more than a running vehicle.

The lawyer struggled to switch gears, making the car look like a sardine can on wheels. William was grateful for the ride, and once he'd paid the tow truck fees, Ariana's lawyer helped him change his tire. After wasting all morning and nearly all afternoon with Ariana, William had no choice but to reschedule his business arrangements. Ariana called Jacqueline, but she had turned off her cell phone.

By the end of the day, Jeff Hurst had managed to persuade the judge that Phil's allegations of insanity were nothing more than an attempt to make Jacqueline suffer. Jacqueline had never stepped into a psychologist's office in her life, and there was obviously no record that could support the allegations. While in court, Jacqueline was assigned a probation officer, who interviewed her to fill out a form about her drinking tendencies.

The officer answered all the questions by making assumptions about Jacqueline's drinking habits. She was now, at least in court papers, classified as having a substance abuse problem. The officer gave her several pamphlets with information about the AA program, behavioral problems, and alcohol. The judge did not remove the restraining order and ordered her to attend AA meetings for ninety days. The restraining order would lose effect in thirty days. Jacqueline had no choice but to accept the sentence.

***

After court, Jeff and Jacqueline stopped at a popular sandwich and soup shop for lunch and conversation. Jeff talked about his children and other trivial family matters.

Jacqueline felt a great weight lift from her shoulders. "Thank you so much for taking my case on such short notice, Jeff."

"It'll turn out all right. You'll see," he said, sipping his tomato soup.

"I just don't understand how Phil could be so evil after so many years of marriage. It's surreal," said Jacqueline, teary-eyed.

"I see it all the time, Jacky. People walk away from marriages all the time. It shouldn't surprise you."

"My parents were happily married for over fifty years. I really thought my marriage could be as happy as theirs."

"You are not your parents, and Phil, as we all know, is not the man you thought."

"He's changed so much."

"We all do, Jacky; the problem is when your personality changes guide you on a different path than your partner's. That's how you grow apart and reach the end."

Jacqueline nodded. Nothing she said or did would change her reality. Phil had changed, had been gone for years despite her reluctance to admit it. This truth had just hit her, and she was drowning in an emotional spiral of loving memories, anger, and helplessness.

Jacqueline got into a yellow cab, and Jeff left on the train. She arrived home to find the place unusually empty. Donna worked quietly, but the boys' absence echoed louder with every passing minute. Thirty days without them would seem like forever, and Jacqueline could only pray to get through the days with her mind intact.

She went to Phil Junior's room and sat in front of the computer to check her email. Surprisingly, there were no replies or emails from the few people she had reached out to. The scant emails were only promotions for some special items from department store boutiques.

None of Phil's friends or their wives had bothered to send her a text message, email, or phone call. Ariana was her only ally. She reflected on how her experience was turning out to be a great teacher. It was helping her learn all too quickly that most of those she had considered friends would take sides with the wealthier, more powerful of the pair.

Jacqueline browsed the internet for information about the AA meetings that she was now condemned to attend but knew nothing about. Her knowledge was limited to what she had seen occasionally in movies or heard in conversation.

After a short while, she changed into something comfortable and brewed herself some tea. She and Donna watched TV in silence until Jacqueline began to share about her experience in court that day.

Donna mentioned a friend who had gone through a similar situation and found a much-needed refuge in yoga. Jacqueline seemed interested. "Today, the lady is a yoga instructor," Donna explained. "It basically saved her life."

"I've always been interested in yoga," said Jacqueline. "I don't know why I haven't taken the time to try it before. I hear nothing but good things."

"I wish I had the time," said Donna. "You should try it."

"Maybe it'll be good for me to take a couple of classes and see how it goes."

"That's right; if nothing else, it'll help keep you calm and balanced throughout this crazy process," Donna said.

Donna had a medical appointment the next morning and would be coming to work a little later than usual. Jacqueline didn't mind and wished her a good night. Before going to bed, Jacqueline helped herself to a small bowl of spaghetti Donna had prepared earlier that day. Just as she was getting ready to lie down, Ariana called.

"Hi, dear. I'm so glad you called," said Jacqueline.

"Where are you?"

"Home—where else?"

"You sound awful. Is everything okay?" asked Ariana.

Jacqueline suddenly realized Ariana knew nothing about the restraining order.

"No, Ari. I'm not okay," she whispered. Taking a deep breath, she continued. "In a nutshell, Phil is gone, he's taken the kids, and I'm getting divorced."

"What?" shrieked Ariana, dumbfounded. "You're shitting me! What happened?"

"I told you, in a nutshell . . . I'll tell you the details tomorrow. I'm exhausted," Jacqueline said.

"Where has he taken the kids? That's kidnapping!"

"No, Ari. He took out a restraining order against me, and I have court-ordered AA meetings," said Jacqueline, getting into bed.

"You? An alcoholic? What a joke! You're the only person I know who wrinkles her face in disgust at a bottle of whiskey!"

"Like I said, I can't get into any details now."

"Well, we'll go to the meetings together then, if you want."

"Sure! That'll probably be the only fun part of this whole process," said Jacqueline, aiming for optimism despite the circumstances. "Are you okay?"

"Actually, no," said Ariana. "Way too much drama."

"What happened?"

"Many things, among which—well, I slept with your friend William."

"Ari! I don't believe you!"

"Well, I don't believe it either, given I don't remember a thing. I just woke up naked in a hotel suite. He was there, so I assume I slept with him," she said.

"Maybe nothing happened."

"Believe me . . . I found myself in a suite at the St. Regis and William was still there. Something did happen."

"No! He paid for a suite at the St. Regis? That's not cheap," said Jacqueline, in awe. Ariana's crazy stories always cheered her up.

"Well, I'm not cheap. Anyway, Carlos canceled all my credit cards."

"Are you kidding?"

"Yes—I mean, no, I'm not kidding. And that's not all . . . Are you ready?"

"Oh my God, what else?" gasped Jacqueline, sitting erect on the edge of her bed.

"That pig canceled all my credit cards, emptied our bank account, and tomorrow I'm out on the street."

"Did you tell your lawyer?" asked Jacqueline.

"Dear, it doesn't matter; these court things take time. Until then, where am I going to stay? I've got no job and four hundred dollars to my name," said Ariana, adopting a tone of serious concern. "I've got to find a job and put the house up for sale. I'm not letting Carlos leave me empty-handed."

Jacqueline thought for a moment, and Ariana kept silent, waiting for suggestions. "Come stay with me, Ari," said Jacqueline. She was confident she could offer a helping hand. Phil was obviously gone and wouldn't be back, ever. She was sure of that. And for the next month, the boys wouldn't be there either.

"Where? At your place?" asked Ariana, and Jacqueline could almost see her smile in relief.

"Yes, stay with me until you can fix your job situation, at least," said Jacqueline. "You can stay in Mark's room. The boys aren't coming back until next month, and Phil will not step foot in this place again while I'm alive.

"You are the absolute best, Jacky."

"Thanks. Now don't worry too much, and go to bed."

"Thanks, Jacky. I'll be the best influence, I promise!"

"No drinking while you're here, that's the only rule."

"You know I don't have an alcohol problem. I only said I did because I wouldn't be caught dead inside a freaking psych ward," Ariana said.

"We'll talk about all this tomorrow."

They wished each other good night, and Jacqueline tucked herself into bed, her head swimming with thoughts of her situation and Ariana's. They shared many undeniable similarities, and since the two of them had been best friends for so long, she found the situation ironic now.

Jacqueline switched off the lights. Her phone blinked, heralding an incoming text message. She smiled at the screen.

"Everything will be fine. I give you my word. Rest well, and trust me, Jeff." His words brought her great comfort, and she realized that deep in her core, she trusted him blindly.

Chapter 6

Jacqueline slept like a baby, unaware of the hustle and bustle that never stopped in the city's streets and subway stations. Meanwhile, nearby, Josefina passed from one car of the moving train to another, anticipating the next stop. The doors opened almost immediately, and passengers rushed out, jostling, as desperate to disembark as wild creatures running from a forest fire.

Unlike the other travelers, Josefina walked calmly with haunted eyes, carrying a backpack with books, half a sandwich, and a small wallet with a few dollars in change. Her pale face contrasted with the dark skin under her eyes, giving her a sickly look.

Josefina had grown up in extreme poverty in a small rural village in the Dominican Republic where most people lacked basic necessities. For Josefina, moving to America had been like a dream come true. She had passed her citizenship exams to become an American citizen, which to her was an accomplishment in itself. After years working double shifts cleaning houses and washing dishes in restaurant kitchens, she was enrolled in a medical assistant program. Her English was poor, but her tenacity and dedication had earned the respect of her classmates and teachers, and she was now just a few weeks shy of graduation.

After escaping the chaotic scene in the train station, she walked a few blocks and stopped at a gray building before entering through the main door. Neither Josefina nor her neighbors cared much that the door knob was broken. The residents knew each other and realized that none of them had anything worth stealing in their apartments.

"Stinks in here!" she remarked as she closed the door behind her. Her dog ran to greet her, shaking his tail excitedly. Nono, Josefina's dog, was a small mutt with a flat, circular snout. She'd rescued the puppy over a year before when she found him abandoned near the staircase in her building. He'd been barely three weeks old, wrapped in an old rag, shaking and sickly. That night, when Josefina took the dog to a nonprofit animal clinic, the vet informed her that he was blind in one eye and had parvovirus. She'd had to leave him there for three days, and when she got him back, she didn't have the heart to let him go.

Josefina fed her dog and left her backpack in her bedroom before returning to the living room, only a few steps away. Her apartment was small and congested, with boxes scattered and stacked on top of one another. Its lack of closet space made it a perfect nightmare for the claustrophobic.

She stood in front of the TV with her arms crossed and glared at her husband, who had been lying there all day. "Johnson . . . you gonna help me or wha?" she scolded in her peculiar accent. "Don't you smell the stink?"

"You're obsessed with cleaning. Like hell I'mma be walking around with a mop . . . C'mon!" he shouted, rolling off the couch and heading to the refrigerator. He grabbed a soda and flopped back down.

"Can you at least walk the dog? I'm busting my ass, working all day and studying all night. All you do is watch TV and won't even help me with the dog!" she pleaded.

"Look, if I walk that wet rat, I'll let him loose! You know I can't stand your fucking dog; you're lucky I haven't thrown it in a ditch somewhere."

What Josefina had initially tolerated as a marriage of convenience, enabling her to get her legal papers, had turned out to be worse than she expected. She and Johnson had little in common, and the sight of him made her stomach turn. Not only had he never been exceptionally romantic, he was mostly emotionally detached, but he had a jealous streak, and she resented him for it. He would seize her phone to rummage through her text messages and contact list like a jealous ogre. He accused her of having imaginary affairs and refused to accept that she preferred to spend her evenings in class rather than lying around at his beck and call.

Josefina's growing ambitions were foreign to Johnson. He was a traditional but closed-minded man. His perspective was about as deep as a puddle, and he was genuinely convinced that a wife belonged in the kitchen or laundry room—or a supermarket, at worst.

Living in a big city had shattered Josefina's limiting beliefs, and she had no place for a man like Johnson in her life now. Her work ethic and dedicated study had lifted her self-esteem, molding her into a strong-minded and opinionated person. Johnson had witnessed firsthand how far she had come. Josefina no longer resembled the shadow she'd been only a few years prior, and he knew that, sooner rather than later, she would gather her possessions and aspirations and walk away.

Johnson jumped from job to job; after managing a pizzeria for less than a year, he'd gone to work at a nightclub as a security guard. He made enough from tips to cover the rent. However, Josefina couldn't tolerate his sporadic tendency to go the extra mile for shady characters. She was glad to be gone most of the day and made sure he knew it. "I made you!" he said.

Josefina shook her head in resignation. Tired of their heated argument, she retreated to the locked bathroom to seek respite in the shower. Her husband ran after her and pounded on the bathroom door.

"I'm leaving! Don't wait up!" he yelled. He changed clothes and left for work.

Josefina stepped out of her haven. She threw on an old T-shirt, a pair of sweatpants, and some warm socks, then threw herself on her bed with a pile of books. She managed to review her notes for a couple of hours that night. As tired as she was, she studied fully alert, concentrating on passing the exams and eager to earn her certificate of completion. Only then would she aim to start a new life with a better-paying job.

***

The following morning, Jacqueline awoke to Ariana's missed calls and only then recalled offering Ariana a place to stay. She stumbled into the kitchen, half asleep, and called Ariana, who had been waiting in the lobby for almost two hours.

Jacqueline called the concierge downstairs to grant Ariana entry, then pulled on a robe just in time to open the door. "Good morning," she said to the valet as he wrestled the cart with Ariana's luggage into the foyer. "What did you bring, your whole house?" teased Jacqueline, sizing up the two large suitcases on the floor. She tipped the valet generously and closed the door behind him.

"What do you mean?" said Ariana defensively. "I'm moving in with you temporarily! What did you think I would bring, a gym bag?"

Jacqueline laughed. "I just thought most of your stuff was still at your house—well, Carlos's house . . ."

"Oh, honey, this isn't even a fourth of my junk. Who knows, maybe it's a good time to give away all the crap I don't need."

"That wouldn't be at all a bad idea," said Jacqueline, dragging one of the suitcases to Mark's bedroom. Ariana followed.

They folded and arranged a few things in the half-empty closet; then Jacqueline gave her a brief tour of the home. Ariana made herself some scrambled eggs while Jacqueline made room to slide the suitcases under the bed. She joined Ariana at the dining table with her usual solitary cup of coffee. Ariana enjoyed a full breakfast.

Ariana elaborated on the details of her court case, which turned out to be more complicated than Jacqueline anticipated. As a friend, Jacqueline shared her concerns. Ariana was reluctant to own her alcoholism and insisted she had only occasional difficulties with her compulsive drinking, the way she struggled to stop eating sweets after eating a chocolate bar. "They wouldn't call me a chocoholic now, would they?" she argued.

Jacqueline shrugged dispiritedly at her remarks and cleared the dishes from the table. It had always been a challenge for Jacqueline to inject sense into Ariana's head. She could only hope that one day Ariana would be honest with herself about her drinking issues.

After breakfast, they took to the internet to search for AA meetings in the city. To their surprise, over a hundred meetings were held every week in different locations. Jacqueline lurched forward in her chair, grinning excitedly.

"Ari, look at this one!" she said, pointing at the computer screen. "This place is only a few minutes away."

"Isn't that near St. Patrick's cathedral?"

"Yes! Isn't that so convenient?" Jacqueline said. "It's only a few minutes' walk from here."

"Jacky, are you nuts?"

"What? Bad idea?" asked Jacqueline, her eyebrows raised.

"We can't afford to be seen at one of those meetings near your neighborhood!"

"Why not?"

"Don't you get it? Jacky! People will stare at us and say, 'Oh, look, the two drunks from those AA meetings near the church.' How embarrassing! That, without question, will kill my credibility as a real estate agent—"

"But those meetings are supposed to be anonymous, right?"

"My God, Jacky. Nobody's anonymous in their own neighborhood."

"Where should we go, then?"

"Let me see . . ." Ariana scanned the website. "Here, Jacky."

Ariana settled on a meeting a hundred blocks away, far enough to assuage her worries. They left the apartment at the height of the morning rush hour. Vacant taxis were nowhere to be found. They soon lost interest in waiting and hurried to the train station. In less than twenty minutes, they had arrived at their destination. Jacqueline followed Ariana like a lost child, and Ariana walked briskly, canvassing her surroundings, consumed by the fear of being spotted by a client or acquaintance.

Ariana was committed to finding a job in the city and knew that this quest would probably consume most of her daytime hours. She concluded that the morning AA meetings would best fit their schedules, and Jacqueline agreed. It would allow her to run errands anytime throughout the day.

The Methodist Church of San Marco, where the AA meeting was being held, was completely empty. Ariana and Jacqueline walked in to find there was nothing going on. Overwhelmed with dismay, Ariana latched onto Jacqueline's arm.

"What's the matter, Ari? You look like you just saw the antichrist."

"I'm outraged!" Ariana wailed.

They sat in the first pew, and Jacqueline wondered if they had gotten the wrong address. Ariana exhaled, rose from the bench, and scanned the room again.

"I don't think there are many alcoholics in this area. This meeting is empty."

"Who's supposed to sign our meeting attendance log?" Jacqueline asked.

"The priest, I think."

"The Methodist church doesn't have priests, Ari!"

"Well . . . maybe their Methodist spiritual guru? How should I know?"

A man entering through a back door interrupted their conversation. Ariana approached him.

"Sir!" she called out, raising her voice.

"Yes? What can I do for you?"

"When does the meeting start?" she asked, agitated.

"We don't have service until noon, ma'am."

"Impossible!" contested Ariana. "We looked up the schedule online and it explicitly stated that there's a meeting every Monday through Friday at eight o'clock. Every morning," she said in a convincing manner while holding out her attendance sheet. The man glanced at the paper and smiled warmly.

"So you're here for the AA meeting, right?"

Jacqueline nodded.

"I apologize. I thought you were referring to our service times. One moment," he said, turning to face the doorway as a woman entered.

"Excuse me!" he called out, waving at the woman.

"Yes?" she replied and approached them.

"These ladies are here to attend the AA morning meeting. Would you happen to know which room the meeting takes place in?"

"Yes, of course! I'm going there, too." The woman extended her hand. "My name is Josefina."

"I'm Ariana, and she's Jacqueline."

"Nice to meet you, Jacqueline. Come with me," said Josefina. "We're already late."

"Better late than never . . ." said Ariana sarcastically.

They walked in and sat in the back row. A man with an impressive beard was leading the meeting that morning. He sat next to a table in the middle of the room. Ariana seemed tense and surveilled the room with wide eyes, like someone trapped in a dark, haunted basement. She couldn't understand how listening to anecdotes from strangers would help anyone abstain from drinking, even for a day. Meanwhile, Jacqueline listened to each member and their stories. For a moment, she had the impression she was part of a secret society, some strange cult.

They wrapped up the one-hour meeting by chanting the serenity prayer, and members trickled toward Jacqueline and Ariana to offer their unconditional support.

Jacqueline found their humility quite moving, and whatever prejudice she harbored toward the group began to rapidly dissipate. Ariana had expected a group of bums and tired-looking people but was pleasantly surprised to see that most of the men there were well dressed, neat, and clean. With the exception of two men who seemed withdrawn and long-faced, everyone was quite extroverted and well mannered. Josefina, Ariana, and Jacqueline were the only three women there, and none of them minded.

Jacqueline and Ariana had spoken with almost every attendee when Josefina introduced them to the man who had led the meeting that morning. Ariana dug the attendance sheet out of her purse and handed it to him. "Someone is supposed to sign our attendance sheet. Would that be you?" she hinted.

The man took the paper. "How did you like the meeting?" he asked.

"I don't know much about this subject. I'm not an alcoholic," said Ariana. "I'm only here because of a court order."

"I thought the meeting was very interesting," interrupted Jacqueline, "but it's hard to form an opinion based on one meeting."

"Why court-ordered?" the man asked, assembling a handful of literature on the subject.

"I just had a hard time one night. I had a few drinks, and well . . . it's a long story."

"We all have long stories," he quipped.

"She got drunk and crashed a car into a house," Jacqueline interjected.

Ariana pulled her aside. "You wanna tell the whole world?"

"You're lucky to be alive," said the man.

"I'm not an alcoholic," Ariana countered nonchalantly.

"You're working on it," said Jacqueline.

The man signed both attendance sheets and handed them back. "Whether you are or aren't an alcoholic is a very personal opinion," he said. "I've been in AA for over thirty years. I can only tell you that nobody makes it into this room by accident."

"I'm not here by mistake; I'm here by a court order," said Ariana.

"Welcome, then. I hope you find it helpful," he said. Before they departed, the man suggested some books

. Josefina chimed in that after being a member for the past three years, she couldn't imagine going back to her old self.

Ariana didn't care to hear anything further about the subject, and it showed. Jacqueline bought a thick blue book and gathered some pamphlets she hoped Ariana would eventually read. They bid farewell to the bearded man and followed Josefina outside.

"I have to be at work in an hour; wanna have coffee with me?" asked Josefina matter-of-factly, hoping to strike up a friendship. Since she was committed to guarding her sobriety, she had no friends outside of AA. Her busy schedule, with work during the day and classes at night, permitted little time for socializing. She did, however, enjoy reaching out to new members to offer support.

"Coffee? Now?" Ariana hesitated. "I don't know . . ."

Jacqueline admired Josefina's relaxed disposition. "Of course. I would love some coffee. Come on, Ari. We have nnothing else to do just now," she concluded, and Ariana agreed.

They sat together at a cafe nearby. Jacqueline ordered green tea, while Josefina and Ariana ordered coffee.

Ariana shared her experience in the psych ward the night she was arrested, and Josefina was not judgmental. She explained that her path to sobriety had not been a smooth one and admitted that the psych ward was a common pit stop for alcoholics. She shared intimately about her life, and her enthusiasm was palpable when she spoke about her upcoming exams and plans for the future. Her honesty and humility made her almost childlike.

The corner booth in the cafe was warm, cozy, and attended by friendly service, making their first encounter with Josefina a memorable moment. They shared their own accounts of their lives and floundering marriages. Jacqueline feared her looming status as a divorcee and confessed she was at a loss for how to start over once the divorce was final. Ariana, on the other hand, expressed concerns about her son, Charley, who was in college and had no idea his father was carrying on a homosexual affair and double life.

Josefina had also been through hell. As a child, she'd survived abuse at the hands of her father and rarely had enough to eat. She confessed that she couldn't imagine anything much worse. She had always been immune to worries. At a young age, she'd learned to look for solutions rather than dwell on her problems. "I'm with Johnson until I finish school," she said. "As soon as I find a good job, I'm out! I can't wait to start from scratch."

Jacqueline stared at her, agape. "Aren't you afraid?" she asked.

Josefina shook her head. "What's the worst that can happen? Think about it—"

"Why haven't you left him? Before now, I mean," Ariana interrupted.

"Because in the program, they tell us to avoid making major life changes during our first year of sobriety."

"But you said you've been sober for three years now, right?" asked Jacqueline, and Josefina nodded.

"Yes, but I figure I've put up with him this long, so waiting one more year until I finish school is no big deal."

"What led you to join AA?" asked Jacqueline, interested.

Josefina leaned forward. "In my last drunken stupor," she whispered, "I came home plastered and caught Johnson with some chick. The second I walked in and saw them on the couch, I cracked. I picked up a broom and smashed his stereo to pieces. He tried to stop me, but I went running after the girl."

"What happened to her?" asked Jacqueline.

"Who cares?" Ariana cut in. "Hopefully, you let her have it. I wish I would've beat the shit out of Johnny with a broom when I found him in bed with Carlos. Actually, forget the broom . . . I would've used a baseball bat!"

"I have no idea how she got away. My memory was toast the next day."

"What a pity," said Ariana.

"I guess men will go as far as you let them," Jacqueline thought out loud, and Josefina nodded.

"He hasn't invited anyone over since then."

"No kidding," said Ariana, and they shared a conspiratorial chuckle.

"That's why I quit drinking. I don't wanna do something crazy that I might regret," confided Josefina.

Jacqueline paid the bill and accompanied Josefina to the train station. "What made you choose that course? I mean, medical assistance?" asked Jacqueline.

"The health business is a sure thing. People never stop getting sick."

"Where do you work now, if you don't mind me asking?" asked Ariana.

"I take care of an old man. He's in a wheelchair. I bathe him, cook for him, do everything for him. I take care of him from ten a.m. until five p.m., and then I go to school. I don't get much sleep."

"I'm sure it'll pay off," Jacqueline assured her. Before leaving, the three women exchanged numbers and agreed to sit together at the AA meeting the next morning.

Jacqueline and Ariana took a cab to the grocery store. It was almost noon when they arrived at the apartment, and Donna was almost done with the housework. Ariana unpacked the rest of her clothes and organized them in the drawers, then joined Donna and Jacqueline for lunch. Donna had prepared lasagna, Jacqueline's favorite. Jacqueline brewed a pot of warm tea and joined Ariana in the living room to enjoy a mystery show on TV.

Soon, Donna joined them, and Jacqueline shared that her experience at the AA meeting that morning had been even better than she anticipated. Ariana agreed but still refused to go near the big blue book or the pamphlets Jacqueline had curated for her. A few hours passed, and Donna wished them good night. It was early evening, and Jacqueline lay on her bed, eager to contact her credit card companies. Luckily, Phil had not yet canceled any of her credit cards, and she was determined to keep it that way.

Ariana knocked just as Jacqueline was getting ready for bed, and when Jacqueline opened the door, Ariana entered, giggling like a little girl and carrying a small red box.

"What's that?" asked Jacqueline. Ariana sat next to her at the foot of the bed but gave no answer.

"What is it?" she asked again.

"It's very personal, but given your situation, I'll share it with you," she whispered as she opened the box. Jacqueline peered curiously at the contents, then frowned. Seconds later, her eyes widened. She gasped and clamped her hands over her mouth, gaping in surprise.

Chapter 7

Jacqueline was startled, almost scandalized, as she rummaged through the contents of Ariana's little red box. It was filled to the brim with the kind of erotic gadgets that might be considered daring to anyone who had never browsed through a sex shop or online store. For Jacqueline, the thought of using anything other than a glass of champagne to arouse herself was nonexistent.

Ariana pulled a blue vibrator from a silk bag and placed it on the bed.

"His name is Joe," she said with genuine enthusiasm.

"Ariana, you know I would never use that . . ."

"It's completely normal!" said Ariana. "I think every woman should have one. Look," she insisted as she grabbed a packaged vibrator from the box. "This one is for you."

"Do you think I would actually enjoy some rubber . . . thing?"

"Why not?"

"Because it's weird! Thanks, Ari, but I'm not that desperate."

"It's okay. You should keep it, just in case you decide to try it sometime."

"I don't think I'll need it."

"Believe me, they work wonders!" exclaimed Ariana.

"Don't you feel strange using it?"

"Not at all! I think it's the greatest thing ever invented for women! You can treat yourself to a pleasurable moment without having to waste time on a lousy date."

"I'd rather waste time on a lousy date."

"Well, of course I'd prefer a hot date. The problem is nice guys are scarce. You know they are."

"That's not true. There's a whole world of nice guys out there waiting to show you a good time, Ari. Surely finding a decent date can't be that difficult."

"Maybe not," said Ariana, "but if you sleep with a guy too soon, he'll think you're too wild. Even nice guys don't like wild."

Jacqueline laughed. Ari was probably right. "Well, I'm sure you know what you're talking about."

"Of course!" said Ariana. She returned her erotic toys to their florid container. "Trust me, that was my experience before Carlos. Actually, he was the only one who stuck around, but of course, we already know Carlos is way different."

"Yes, that he is."

Ariana replaced the lid on her little red box. Jacqueline snatched it from her and took out one of a few gel bottles.

"What's this one for?" she asked, giggling conspiratorially.

"That's some marvelous oil. It turns warm when you rub it on the skin. It feels fantastic. If you ever need a good massage, it's actually great for that too," said Ariana, tossing it back into the box.

"What do you mean? What else would you use it for?" asked Jacqueline.

Ariana shook her head. "Never mind, Jacky . . . It would just make you blush."

"What do you mean? I wouldn't mind trying it."

"Absolutely not. The last thing we need is for you to jump out of bed, scared out of your wits, and call 911, freaked out at your own orgasm—"

Jacqueline laughed at this image. "Oh . . . I wouldn't use it like that," she said, reddening.

Regardless of how many years had gone by, Ariana and Jacqueline's views on sexuality and relationships were worlds apart. Ariana did enjoy having Jacqueline as close as two friends could be but perceived her old-fashioned ways as an inexcusable obstacle to exploring her own intimacy. At their age, she would expect Jacqueline to be more accepting of her silly toys, but she realized that such things offended Jacqueline's puritanical sensibilities. Ariana was disenchanted to see Jacqueline was as sexually reserved as she had always been.

Ariana good-naturedly wished Jacqueline good night and locked herself in her own room. Shortly afterward, she received the call from her banker friend. He was in Indonesia, closing negotiations to finance several projects, and promised to meet with her when he returned. Ariana was anxious to return to work, and when she explained her precarious situation, he offered to introduce her to the manager of a reputable brokerage firm in the city. At least she could place her real estate license with them for a short time and learn more about the business in the city before moving on.

Jacqueline lay in bed. After twisting and turning for a while, she sat up and browsed through a fashion magazine, hoping to clear her mind. When she finally began to feel sleepy, she tossed the magazine on the floor and reached for the light switch. At that moment, her lawyer called.

"Hi, Jacky. Sorry about the time," he apologized.

"Hi, Jeff. No worries. What's going on? Is everything okay?" she asked inquisitively.

"Yes, but I just looked at the emails you sent me. There's not much we can do with those."

Days prior, Jacqueline had sent Jeff a thread of emails that exposed a conversation between Phil and his mistress. Jeff explained to Jacqueline that the only email that could compromise Phil was not good enough. In that email, Phil agreed to meet his mistress to look at an apartment, but they never mentioned any details about whose apartment that was or the reason for their meeting, and the conversation did not implicate either of them. If she couldn't furnish solid evidence of the affair, her accusations would be explained away by his attorney, and most likely dismissed.

"I don't have anything else, Jeff," she admitted, choking up.

"Can you get a hold of any credit card statements?" he asked.

Unfortunately, she could not. Phil's personal mail had been delivered to his office for the past couple of years. When he went on short trips or traveled abroad, he always used his corporate accounts, which she had no access to. He left no trail.

Jeff assured Jacqueline that he had hired a private investigator to work on her case. She would have to cover that cost, but she didn't mind. If the investigator was as good as Jeff suggested, surely they could scrape together clear evidence of Phil's ongoing affair.

Jeff told Jacqueline that Phil already knew about her false claim of drunkenness on the night she cut his clothes into shreds. Phil's accusations regarding Jacqueline's mental issues didn't hold water in court. In her defense, Jacqueline had no history of substance abuse, and even her doctor knew she was not fond of medications. She hated to take pills and only begrudgingly accepted prescribed antibiotics to treat a minor infection or something worst. Calcium chews and multivitamins were, in her opinion, the keys to good health.

Phil was surprised by Jacqueline's competent counterattack. Having Jeff as her attorney would make the divorce proceedings an uphill battle for him. Jeff knew more about Phil than Phil would've cared to admit, and that alone put him at a great disadvantage. To get Phil to cool down and back off, Jeff warned his attorney that he had some compromising evidence against Phil, and when pressed, he refused to surrender any details. Jeff acknowledged that what little evidence he had wouldn't make the divorce settlement an open-and-shut case. Phil was now on his toes, apprehensive about the alleged evidence against him.

Jacqueline thanked Jeff for hiring a private investigator, and they made plans to meet the following week. She lay silently in her bed and contemplated the way things were unfolding. She couldn't understand how or why she still had mixed feelings about going through with her divorce.

A moment of clarity shook her senses. From that moment on, she wouldn't experience the uncertainty she'd lived through countless times in the past when calling Phil's office in an attempt to get his attention. Those moments had dominated her daily routine only days before. Often, she'd found herself in a dark, unsettling place; paranoia overwhelmed her on the rare occasions when Phil deigned to answer her calls. In such cases, she held her breath, consumed by determination to hear the slightest background noise that might betray his whereabouts, with a painful churning in the pit of her stomach. That agonizing sensation had become commonplace, especially in the wee hours of the night. Jacqueline closed her eyes, basking in the absence of that agony. For the first time in a long time, she drifted into a deep sleep, enveloped in the calm that only true peace could bring. It was time to stay optimistic and look ahead to a new life of embracing her new self at last.

The next day, Jacqueline and Ariana went to the AA meeting feeling less inhibited. They listened to the stories, and unbeknownst to Jacqueline, Ariana harbored less inner conflict than before. She could find commonality with the other members, based on their anecdotes, and felt that perhaps she could use some information about the program. She told herself to keep an open mind. She still declined to speak but was pleased to be in the room. The hour-long meeting passed quicker than she expected.

Josefina arrived late, looking worn out, agitated, and absentminded. After the meeting, she joined Jacqueline and Ariana at the same cafe they had visited the day before. They sat in the same booth and enjoyed a candid conversation. Jacqueline noted that Josefina didn't seem well, and she asked why. Josefina hesitated before sharing her concerns.

"I'm stressed out," she said. "The old man I work for is very sick."

Josefina had little appetite that morning and nibbled slowly on a small piece of toast.

"Did he fire you?" asked Ariana, intrigued. Josefina shook her head.

"No," she said. "He's in the hospital, in a room full of wires and machines—"

"Do you mean the intensive care unit?" probed Jacqueline in complicity.

"Yes, that's what it is. His skin is yellow. He's been sleeping for three days now. His daughter told me that she will only need me to work half a day."

"Is he that ill?" asked Ariana.

Jacqueline poured Josefina some more coffee and smiled warmly. "Well, he's very old. You mentioned that yesterday."

Josefina nodded. "Yes, he's eighty-six . . ."

"Good lord!" said Ariana. "I wouldn't wanna live that long. Can you imagine? What a nightmare—having to wake up and look at my wrinkled face and useless body in the mirror every morning. I would hang myself—"

"Jesus, Ari. I can't believe the things that come out of your mouth!" said Jacqueline.

"I don't know," Josefina continued. "I know he's not doing very well, but I really need him to come out of that machine room—"

"It's not your fault! The man is old! What can you do?" Ariana blurted out.

Jacqueline laid her hand on Ariana's arm. "Ari, it's not about blaming anyone. If the man dies, she'll be out of a job," she explained softly.

"Oh!" said Ariana. "Well, in that case, I'm sure you can always find another old man. It shouldn't be that difficult."

Josefina explained that jobs like hers were hard to come by and the families often expected caregivers to stay overnight and work without schedule restrictions. Josefina was almost done with her course and had to study for exams. She had no time to go job hunting, even if she wanted to.

The old man's daughter had reduced her working hours, and Josefina agonized, knowing she would be short on what was already reduced income. The old man's family hoped he'd recover promptly, but based on his condition, their expectations seemed low.

"I imagine his daughter could perhaps help you for the next week, right?" Ariana asked.

Josefina shook her head, and Ariana rolled her eyes.

"Bitch!" she spat.

"What about your husband? Wouldn't he help you in this situation?" asked Jacqueline.

Josefina smiled. "No, he never helps me with money," she said. "He pays the rent and makes sure to remind me of it every day."

"What a jerk," said Ariana.

"Stop it, Ari," Jacqueline scolded. She turned to Josefina. "So what's your plan?"

"Study and hope the old man makes it through. I'll be graduating in a couple of weeks, and the school helps us with job placement."

"Then it's not so bad," said Ariana. Josefina smiled halfheartedly and shrugged. She explained that there was a waiting list for job placement and some people had to wait as long as a year. Luckily for her, she didn't owe money for tuition. She had received a grant and her church had helped pay for books and other materials. But a cut in her earnings would mean being a burden on her husband, who would have to cover other housing expenses like groceries and cable on top of the rent, which he already did. She couldn't bear the thought. Things were bad already.

"I have to work. I don't have a choice," she sighed. "Johnson only complains and complains. I need to work to save money so I can leave. I'm miserable."

"You can always sit with him and have that talk," said Jacqueline.

"What talk?" asked Josefina.

"Try to sit calmly and have a heart-to-heart talk. Perhaps you guys could work things out, and if he's willing to change even a little, you might have a chance to save your marriage." Johnson was not a drinker and Jacqueline wanted to believe the womanizing issues could always be resolved. "Sooner or later, they tire of it," she said, attempting to convince herself as much as Josefina. Almost immediately, she retracted her statement, admitting that she wasn't particularly qualified to give such advice.

They said their goodbyes, and Josefina headed to the school library to catch up on her studies. Jacqueline and Ariana stopped by the apartment. Jacqueline was eager to enroll in a yoga studio, and she invited Ariana, who was not fond of breaking a sweat. Nevertheless, Ariana suspected that a visit to the yoga studio could be, if only for an hour, an interesting adventure.

As they walked to a studio only six blocks from Jacqueline's place, Ariana complained to Jacqueline about her depressing circumstances.

"Jacky, after so many years and mothering his child, can you believe that Carlos canceled all my cards? I don't even have enough to cover the cost of public transportation! Four hundred dollars—that's all I have to my name."

"If you like the class, I'll treat you to one month's membership. This yoga thing might just be good for us," said Jacqueline.

"Yeah, if I don't have a nervous breakdown in the middle of the first class."

The short walk led them to the double doors of the yoga studio. Jacqueline approached the young man behind the counter. He welcomed them with a tall glass of mint tea, then launched into an explanation of the different membership packages. Jacqueline purchased a one-month membership and was glad to have the option of getting a full week pass for Ariana. Knowing her, a one-month commitment was likely a waste of money. Jacqueline had the hunch that her friend Ariana would tag along for a while but wouldn't last.

"All right, Ari, here's your one-week pass," announced Jacqueline, feeling a sense of accomplishment. She handed Ariana the weekly pass, and Ariana shoved it into her purse.

"I don't know about yoga, Jacky. You might just find it more fulfilling to do your bending and twisting absolutely solo—"

"You don't know that yet, Ariana. Quit complaining."

"How can yoga benefit me? Besides teaching me to breathe better and stretch a little?" Ariana asked the guy behind the counter, and he stepped out and approached them.

"First time?" he guessed. "It helps to detox, to stretch. It can also improve your posture—"

"Okay, okay . . . I'll try it," interrupted Ariana. She sounded disconnected and totally uninterested.

They unrolled their mats and sat down, ready to start. A young man near the front of her mat tapped Ariana on the shoulder.

"Come. I want to show you ladies the class next door. It's an advanced class," he said. "Some of those ladies are like sixty or seventy years old!" He managed to arrest both Jacqueline and Ariana's attention, and now they were eager to see the yoga practitioners next door.

They followed him a few feet away to a large glass window

Ariana gawked at the three women and two old men who appeared over fifty, but their exact ages were indeterminate. They twisted and turned their bodies like rubber.

"How old are those two women?" asked Ariana.

"Oh, that's Kathy and Pat. They're in their late sixties. We do movie nights sometimes; they're fun," he said.

Ariana was attracted by the idea of aging with the flexibility of a twenty-year-old.

"Did you hear that, Jacky?" she whispered as they walked back to their mats. "Can you imagine?"

"No, actually, I can't," said Jacqueline, but Ariana persisted.

"In a night of passion, with that flexibility? Honey, I could be good enough at sixty for any cute thirty-year-old."

Jacqueline chuckled. "Ari, I'm sure you'd have little in common," she said, shocked at the idea.

Ariana tried to keep up with the class, but after twenty minutes, she had to be escorted out by one of the instructors. They followed a style called Bikram yoga, and the room was kept at ninety degrees. Ariana had taken a diuretic the night before and, after nearly fainting and making a scene, she was convinced that yoga was more complicated than she'd expected.

At the end of the class, Jacqueline found Ariana sitting near the reception desk, drinking a cold bottle of Gatorade.

"I guess you won't be coming with me tomorrow," Jacqueline joked.

"Sure I can! If you wanna roll me out on a gurney afterward, count me in!" she said, and they both laughed.

The afternoon flew by, and at nightfall, Ariana received a text from William. He greeted her casually, and she could not understand why, after all the grief she had caused the man, he would consider communicating with her again. He extended a dinner invitation and she accepted. He was in Wisconsin on business and assured her that he would call her when he made it back from his trip.

Ariana popped some popcorn and joined Jacqueline on the couch to watch TV.

"Is that Will you're texting?" asked Jacqueline with a knowing smile.

Ariana handed over her phone. Jacqueline read their conversation with amusement.

"Whoa! You must've done something right, but watch out, Ari. Don't go too far . . ."

"Whatever," said Ariana as Jacqueline handed her phone back.

"I mean it!" said Jacqueline "You don't know this guy, regardless of how nice he seems. Besides, I heard somewhere that it's best to stay single for at least a year after a divorce."

"Ah, Jacky, sure. I'll make a note."

"You don't know Will. Besides, I don't see him as a perfect match for you. I feel like he's hiding something . . . Ari."

"Okay, so I'll just say, 'Excuse me, but sorry! I'm waiting for Mr. Right, who may or may not come around sometime in my next life, cause in this one I'm simply shit out of luck—'"

"I'm just giving you advice, that's all. Do what feels right to you."

"I will, okay? And don't worry so much about me."

The shock of discovering her husband's homosexual affair had traumatized Ariana to the point that she no longer cared about formality in relationships. Opening up to any man, trusting any man enough to start a life together all over again, was unimaginable.

They ended the conversation on that note. As different as the two of them were, they balanced each other perfectly. Ariana complained about her wine cravings but refrained from drinking with the help of some antianxiety medications. She preferred to abstain, knowing she could be screened by her probation officer anytime. Jacqueline's support also helped Ariana control her anxiety, especially since they kept busy every day.

Ariana's attorney called her that night to let her know that he was setting everything up for her perfectly. Carlos seemed to have a guilty conscience about everything that had happened and explained to Ariana's lawyer that he did not feel ready to meet with her in person yet. Ariana also agreed that keeping their distance would be best, at least for the moment. Her lawyer would be meeting with Carlos's attorney soon, and then she would know what to expect from him. She felt relieved.

Chapter 8

The dynamics and stories in the AA meetings captivated Jacqueline, and after she shared her views on them, and on the so-called disease of alcoholism, even Ariana seemed intrigued by the subject. Although Ariana had grown more accepting of the group and come to attribute her miraculous sobriety to her daily presence at the meetings, she still suffered from the tug-of-war in her mind. She preferred to blame her reckless drinking on her compulsive nature and not some undiagnosed disease. She told herself that if she could limit her drinking, she would eventually be able to enjoy a social outing and drink like any normal person.

Jacqueline enjoyed long afternoon strolls through Central Park three times a week, and taking yoga classes had turned out to be therapeutic. Her divorce case progressed slowly in court. Phil was granted his petition to extend the restraining order for fourteen days, but the surplus of free time away from Phil and the chaos of bringing up two boys enlightened her about how much of life she had been missing. She was no longer obsessed with preserving her relationship and regretted the many chances she had given her husband to save their irreparable marriage. It was clear now that Phil was hopeless and her marriage had no chance at all.

Visits to the cafe across the street from the Methodist church after the AA morning meetings had become routine. One of those mornings during breakfast, Jacqueline asked Josefina why she had been so withdrawn. Josefina forced a smile and seemed tense, realizing that everyone had noticed. She shared her overwhelming sadness, describing to Jacqueline and Ariana her increasingly miserable life at home.

"Johnson slapped me last night," she confided, holding back tears.

"What happened?" asked Jacqueline, holding her hand gently.

Ariana gawked, her cup of steaming hot coffee hovering in midair. "You're shitting me, right?"

Josefina shook her head.

"Why did he slap you?" Jacqueline asked again in her usual soft voice.

"We were arguing, and I complained about him being home all day doing nothing. Then I joked that I make enough money to hire him to walk my dog, and he slapped me."

"Is he mentally unstable?" asked Jacqueline.

Ariana leaned forward. "Has he done it before?"

Josefina shook her head.

Ariana gazed at her with big eyes. "Then what the hell happened? Did you ask him?"

"No, he left and still wasn't home this morning. He's usually home from the club by the time I get ready to leave."

"Some men can't handle it when their wives make something of themselves," said Jacqueline, "but he's gone too far now."

"Totally agree. I think you're gonna have to sit down with the jerk and have 'the talk,'" said Ariana.

"He won't even go to the supermarket. I have to do the grocery shopping and laundry on my only day off, all by myself!"

"That bastard," spat Ariana. "That's it . . . if I were you, I'd sit his flat ass down and have a little chat."

"What kind of chat?" asked Josefina.

"When you tell him he'd better change or you're going to dump his sorry ass. That kinda talk."

"Please, Ari. Do you have to be so abrasive?" Jacqueline scolded.

"Me? Abrasive? I'm not the one sitting in my underwear, watching soap operas and slapping my wife around! He's a loser. I say you dump him!"

"Well, Ari might be right . . ."

"What do you mean?" asked Josefina, clearing her throat.

Jacqueline leaned closer. "Men shape up quickly when they're threatened with separation or divorce."

"Yup! More often than not," said Ariana. Jacqueline nodded in agreement.

Josefina took their advice to heart and promised she would consider shaking things up. She perceived them as worldly and was convinced that if they advised her with such conviction, they were probably right, even though Josefina wondered why they themselves never followed their own advice. She thought that they had given their input based on their own experience by advising her to do what they themselves should've done.

They left the cafe, and Jacqueline rushed to the sidewalk, hailing a cab. Josefina was headed to drop off a job application, and Jacqueline offered her a lift. Ariana joined them in the cab and asked to be dropped off at the train station nearest Times Square. She had arranged to meet her lawyer nearby. Jacqueline went straight to Jeff's office for an early meeting and greeted him warmly when she arrived. He was unenthusiastic, and she found his bland welcome strange. She sat in a chair facing his desk and wondered at his gaunt appearance.

"My god, Jeff, are you okay?"

"Yes. We're remodeling the apartment, and, well . . . my wife has gone a little overboard with the spending. I'm trying to cut corners, and just when I'm about to clear some debt, she goes off the rails with credit cards and other unexpected and unnecessary purchases," he said, sounding apologetic for her.

"I completely understand," sympathized Jacqueline. "It's always a challenge to remodel a place on a tight budget."

Jeff nodded and shrugged his shoulders in resignation. The tragic reality was that his wife had been a shopaholic for years. In the past week alone, she had blown over fifty thousand dollars. He was a patient man and tried to encourage her to control her budget and refrain from unnecessary spending. In the past, he had sent her to a counselor to undergo intense therapy for her compulsive shopping, but to no avail. She broke all her promises and reverted to her old ways. He worked incessantly to provide for her and for their two children, who were about to enter college.

When Jeff had deactivated her credit card, nearly a year before, his wife got a hold of their savings account and squandered nearly a quarter of a million dollars on art, jewelry, and designer bags. As much as he loved her, he was convinced that this lapse had been the last straw and feared that soon they would face divorce. He was not soothed by talking about his problems at home and preferred to focus on his work. It helped him escape from his personal reality.

"How do you feel, Jacky?"

"I'm all right. Ariana is staying with me for a while, at least a couple of weeks, and of course, her company helps. But I really miss my boys. Have you heard anything from Phil's attorney?"

"Yes, actually. I spoke to him earlier today. I made it clear that should Phil demean you in front of your children, well . . . that could be considered parental alienation, and he could find himself in real trouble."

"Jeff, that's my worst fear—that Phil might vilify me to my boys."

"He won't" he said. "I spoke to your caseworker, and she told me to remind you to get your attendance sheet signed each time you attend those meetings. Your boys might need some counseling too, just so you're aware." Jacqueline nodded, and he smiled. "Very well, then," he said. "The restraining order ends on Thursday. You'll get your kids back then."

"I don't think I can ever forgive Phil for this," Jacqueline said. "For the trauma all this chaos might have caused them. He's a despicable man." She wiped away tears. "I'll take the kids to a therapist when the divorce is final."

Jeff stood, and she followed him to the door. "I think it would be best to take them both as soon as you can. Children are usually affected in the process of divorce, and even more so after it's finalized. Besides, splitting your assets can be a tedious process, and based on what we know so far, well . . . it might be a while before everything is resolved with Phil," said Jeff.

"What do you mean?"

"Friday, we'll meet with Phil and his attorney. The restraining order expires on Thursday. We'll see what they bring to the table then. I'll ask for alimony plus child support. Compile a list of your assets, you know, real estate and all. Email it to my office as soon as it's done. I'll take a look at it and make a draft for the proposal."

"All right. I'll make that list over the weekend," she agreed. Jeff held the door open.

"I'll go over the list as soon as I get it, and if I have any questions, I'll let you know," he assured her.

Jacqueline hugged him in relief. The divorce battle had started. Though she didn't mention it to Jeff, she was now terrified by the prospect of facing a whole new world alone. In the moment, she failed to consider that in her loveless marriage, she had always been lonely. Until that moment, Jacqueline had dealt with the separation in a semi-conscious state, as though lost in a fuzzy dream.

Jeff perceived her sadness and squeezed her shoulders benevolently. "Jacky," he said, "this whole ordeal will end soon. You'll be much better off. I promise."

Jacqueline thanked him for his support. They went their separate ways, and that afternoon she arrived home after dark. When she walked in, she found Ariana lying on the sofa, unusually delighted at her return.

"Hi, darling!" Ariana exclaimed, rushing to hug her before she made it past the foyer. "How was your meeting with Jeff?"

"It went well. Soon this nightmare will be over. I may just need a vacation then," Jacqueline exhaled, removing her coat, then her shoes. She went to her room and undressed, then slipped a robe on and drew a hot bath with aromatic oils. Ariana followed her into the bedroom and sat on the loveseat at the foot of the bed.

"Can you believe what he's doing?"

"Who? Carlos? What did he do now?" asked Jacqueline from the bathroom as she stepped into the warm, scented water.

"My lawyer told him that I wanna sell the house, and, well, that asshole wants to keep the house and buy me out! Can you believe it?"

"But that's a good thing. You'll have money to start from scratch and buy something for yourself."

"That's not the point! Carlos is staying! He's gonna be living under my roof with my cousin Johnny! How humiliating!"

"What do you care? Don't get fixated on controlling everything, Ari. Let it go. Really. I know it's hard, but give yourself a chance to forgive and forget."

"What will the neighbors say? This is so embarrassing to me," stressed Ariana.

"Embarrassing for them, not for you. They'll be the ones who have to face the neighbors after all this, not you."

"When you put it that way, maybe you're right," said Ariana. "And what about you? What's going on? With the divorce, I mean. Any news?"

"Jeff asked me to make a list of all our assets and stuff."

"I can help you with that, if you want."

"No, it's okay. I got it," said Jacqueline, feeling pressed to change the subject. "Have you heard from Will?"

"Yes. He's taking me to Le Cirque tomorrow for dinner," she said triumphantly.

"That's my favorite," said Jacqueline, rising from the tub and swaddling herself in a fluffy towel. "The man has good taste."

"I made the reservation. He has no clue." Ariana said proudly.

Jacqueline snickered. "You're so naughty, Ari. He'd do better than that. Can I advise you not to drink?"

"You can, but I can't promise I'll take your advice."

"You really are a lost cause."

"I haven't had a drop of alcohol since we started going to the AA meetings, so cut me some slack."

"As you wish," conceded Jacqueline, tying her bathrobe around her.

Jacqueline ambled to the kitchen and made a cup of green tea. Ariana mentioned that she had missed several calls from Josefina that evening, but when she tried to call back, her calls went straight to voicemail. Ariana was anxious, suspecting that something bad may have happened.

Jacqueline advised her not to worry. They would catch up with Josefina the next morning, and whatever the situation, if it wasn't pressing enough to merit a call back, Jacqueline was certain it could wait. Ariana was satisfied with this reasoning, and they wished each other good night before curling up in their respective beds for a long, deep sleep.

The next morning, Jacqueline opened her eyes with a start and glanced intuitively at her cell phone screen.

"We're late!" she shouted, jumping out of bed.

Ariana had just awakened as well and got ready in a hurry. Soon they walked out of the building and flagged down a cab. They entered the meeting half an hour late, but the other attendees, engrossed in the story being shared, didn't notice. At the end of the meeting, Jacqueline approached Josefina, who had taken a seat in a corner of the room and had been unusually quiet that morning. Ariana greeted her with a warm hug and noticed her tired, woebegone countenance.

"You don't look well," Jacqueline said.

Josefina forced a smile. "I called last night, Jacky. I called you both," she said, lifting a large bundled sheet from the floor.

"I'm sorry," said Jacqueline. "My phone was dead. Ari mentioned it last night."

"I saw that you called, and tried calling you back a few times, but it went straight to voice mail. What happened? What's that you're carrying?" asked Ariana.

"I followed your advice. I told Johnson I wanted a divorce."

"And what happened?" asked Jacqueline apprehensively.

"He dragged me to the bedroom by my hair and started throwing all my stuff outside. I was terrified. I thought he was gonna kill me! I just threw everything on the bedsheet and ran to my neighbor's. She let me stay with her until morning."

"You could've called the cops!" said Ariana. Jacqueline agreed, but Josefina shook her head.

"Jesus, there's no way I would've called knowing that he would be taken to jail. I'd have to go to court eventually, and I don't have time for that. Besides, he's moving all his stuff out of the apartment as we speak. I don't need police trouble in the middle of my exams."

"You can stay in the apartment then, right? Let him leave!" said Ariana.

"No. We owe three months' worth of overdue rent that he never told me about. He's obviously been planning to move out for a while, but I didn't notice because I've been so busy with my classes. I had no idea he stopped paying the rent. As soon as I told him I wanted a divorce, he lost it, then said I have to leave because he's already moving out. He'll be returning the keys to our landlord before five tonight."

"I'm so sorry I told you to drop him like the scum of the earth that he is. Where can you go?" asked Ariana.

"It was bound to happen, Ariana. I had to leave him eventually. It's not your fault," Josefina reassured her, walking toward the door with the bundled sheet over her shoulder.

"Where are you going now?" asked Jacqueline.

"I'll talk to the minister. Hopefully he can help me find a place."

Josefina had no family in the city, and now, unless she found a place to stay, she'd have nowhere to sleep, shower, or eat, and having a dog at her side only complicated an already devastating situation.

"This is Nono," said Josefina, petting the dog she had tied to a leash in the entrance doorway. Earlier that morning, she'd taken the time to explain her situation to the management. The minister knew her well, and they allowed her to leave the dog there without complaint.

"Nono," Jacqueline acknowledged, watching the dog flutter excitedly.

An assistant from the church approached them and handed Josefina a list of shelters for the homeless. He also gave her a list of other nonprofit organizations that offered room and board to battered women. He had called some battered women's shelters while Josefina was in the AA meeting that morning because he believed they would suit her better than a homeless shelter, but now he stood at the entrance of the church with a drawn look. As Josefina drew near, she suspected he would not be the bearer of good news. She was right. There were no vacancies. Now

Josefina had no choice but to choose from the list of homeless shelters. When the man explained that she'd have to arrive at the shelters before seven in the evening if she hoped to get a bed, she lamented that it was not possible because her classes weren't over until ten.

Ariana stared pointedly at Jacqueline and pulled her aside.

"Jacky—the poor woman, she's on the street," Ariana whispered. Jacqueline silently watched Josefina talk shyly with the man about the nearest homeless shelter.

"I know," Jacqueline exhaled. She contemplated Josefina's dire situation for a moment, then approached them. "Come stay with us," she suggested. "At least until you're done with your classes next week. I'm sure Ariana can make a few calls in the meantime and help you find a place."

"Really?" replied Josefina, surprised.

Jacqueline nodded. "I'm sure you'll get a job by then."

"What about my dog?" asked Josefina in a shaky voice.

"Just make sure he doesn't pee inside the apartment."

Josefina agreed, explaining that she had successfully trained him to wet on disposable pads, and Jacqueline was relieved.

"At least your pet is a sweet puppy, unlike Jacky's ex-dog, Phil!"

Jacqueline ashook her head at this wisecrack, not at all surprised. Ariana had despised Phil since hearing of his first affair nearly fifteen years before. Afterward, she had encountered him and one of his many mistresses outside a restaurant frequented by Wall Street bankers. She had no incentive to hold back and made a scene in broad daylight. Since that day, Phil couldn't stand the sight of her any more than she could stand him.

Jacqueline, Ariana, and Josefina left the church and an unusually long cab ride, they walked inside. Jacqueline's building. Josefina was awestruck at the exquisite elegance of the lobby, which was filled with the kind of luxury she had seen only in movies. She looked around mesmerized, her face tense.

The valet took Josefina's belongings. In a matter of minutes, they were walking through the door of Jacqueline's apartment as the valet followed from the service elevator.

Ariana showed Josefina to Phil Junior's room, and after a brief tour of the place, Josefina took a few minutes to arrange some of her things in the only two empty drawers in the nightstand. She retrieved a disposable bed pad and water and food dishes from her backpack and searched for the right location to arrange a corner for her pet.

"Where's the bathroom?" she asked Ariana.

"That door, right in the middle of the hallway."

Josefina walked down the hallway to set up her dog's space. She scanned each corner of the bathroom. There was an indescribable difference between her mold-splattered, unventilated bathroom and that extravagant room with its shiny marble walls, golden faucets, and glittery accessories. Josefina was dumbfounded but felt strangely comfortable despite the opulence around her.

"This place is amazing!" she gushed. "How many hours do you have to work to pay for a place like this?" she asked Jacqueline in the hallway.

"I don't know, dear. My husband bought it, but I know that the maintenance alone is quite expensive. If I had to pay for it, I would rather get a large house in the countryside," Jacqueline said in an attempt to downplay the pomposity of her lifestyle. Josefina was impressed by her humility although, despite being unaware of it, Jacqueline was always proper and dignified without seeming snobbish.

Josefina lingered in the kitchen and chatted with Donna, who had greeted her graciously and was glad to take a break when Josefina insisted on cooking for everyone. She arranged the dining table beautifully and served a variety of flavorful dishes that were traditional in her native Dominican Republic. After a hearty late lunch, Donna brewed some coffee and served dessert, and the conversation turned to recipes, life changes, and childhood memories. Jacqueline, Ariana, and Donna were shocked to hear about the squalor in Josefina's homeland. The government was so corrupt that it barely provided the necessary resources and infrastructure for schools or education. Josefina described the public hospitals' lack of basic supplies to stitch a deep cut or treat wounds. Donna speculated that Josefina could be right but was perhaps exaggerating, but Jacqueline's heart went out to her, and to all the poor Dominicans in rural areas.

Jacqueline talked about Phil and her children and shared that Jeff had assured her the restraining order would expired on Thursday. Her boys would be home then. Ariana had not yet found a steady job and expressed her concerns. Jacqueline insisted that their temporary stay would not be a problem because the boys could share a room and Josefina and Ariana could do the same. Both of the boys' bedrooms had sofa beds, which Jacqueline had used occasionally when the boys had sleepovers.

The old man that Josefina worked for had died the previous night. She had gotten the call earlier that morning and was now completely out of work. The old man's daughter offered to cover two weeks' pay, and Josefina was grateful to have a bit of dependable income until school ended and she was able to find another job.

Jacqueline urged her to focus on the exams; surely she would soon have a better chance of finding a medical assistant job. The old man's daughter also offered Josefina a good letter of recommendation, understanding that to care for the elderly, she would very well need it.

"I appreciate you letting me stay with you for these few days," said Josefina.

"Don't worry, Josefina. I'm sure we can help you find something in the meantime, until you finish class and get your certificate of medical whatever, and all that," said Ariana.

"I could clean someone's house for a few hours in the morning while I'm waiting," said Josefina. "I really wouldn't mind. Besides, I can find a room to rent soon, in my neighborhood. I don't know what I'll do about my dog."

"Don't worry about that right now," said Jacqueline. "Just focus on passing your exams. One thing at a time, otherwise you'll lose your mind."

Ariana nodded in agreement.

"It's funny," said Ariana. "The lady I sold the funeral home to a year ago called me just a few days ago, asking if I knew anyone who could work at her funeral home."

"My god, Ari. Doing what? Working with corpses could be traumatic," said Jacqueline.

Josefina shook her head. "I think working with the living is worse than working with the dead!" she said playfully.

"Have you ever worked at a funeral? Or a vigil?" asked Ariana. Josefina hadn't, but she admitted that her only experience at a vigil had been when her brother's wife died of cancer a few years before.

She had traveled to the Dominican Republic to help her brother and family members with the funeral arrangements. Josefina's brother and his in-laws made some beautiful flower arrangements and the sisters of the deceased had dressed her beautifully in a long white gown that made her look more like a bride in a deep sleep than a lifeless body in a casket. The nearest funeral home was almost an hour away and the family could not afford the transportation or a proper service. In that village, families traditionally held vigils in their homes, and Josefina's sister in-law's vigil was no different. Friends and neighbors stopped by to express their condolences.

The day of the vigil, the girl's mother cooked a large pot of stew. Relatives gathered the necessary ingredients to cook a simple but large meal, enough for more than twenty people. It was a heartwarming tradition to feed those paying their respects to the dead, and Josefina watched as the people stood in line with their empty plates, waiting to be served. When Josefina asked her brother about the unusually long line, he confessed that his wife had been quite reserved. Josefina had never known her sister-in-law to be chatty or friendly, and her brother agreed that most of the attendees were only there to be fed.

Josefina noticed that some people would approach the casket, which sat right in the middle of the living room. She informed her brother that she would not sleep under the same roof, only steps away from her late sister-in-law's lifeless body. It had been over a day, and the smell was penetrating the walls and beginning to putrefy the space. After much persuasion, her brother agreed and with the help of a friend, they carried the casket to the back porch.

Ariana was less than sensitive as usual, pronouncing it an uncivilized tradition, and Josefina agreed. Jacqueline thought it would be, at least for her, nothing short of a culture shock. Josefina had worked and sent money to her family every month for years, but freely admitted that she could never move back to her old village. Her experience in America had changed her to the extent that even the mentality of the people from her village seemed too primitive now.

Ariana helped clear the plates from the table and sat down again. She patted Josefina's hand. "I just sent a message to my client," she said. "Hopefully she still needs someone to work at the funeral home."

"Christ had mercy when I ran into you two," said Josefina shyly.

"It's fine, girl. You'll be all right."

Jacqueline excused herself and called the concierge to relay Josefina's information so they would grant her entry regularly that week. She gave instructions and explained the basic protocol to Josefina in case she was ever confronted when entering the building, and Josefina expressed her gratitude. Soon, it was time for her to freshen up and head to class.

Ariana cleared the remaining dishes and helped Donna put everything away.

That evening, Ariana spoke to her attorney. He informed her that since she had few assets other than her home and a car that was not paid for and was only in Carlos's name, her divorce case would be simple. Her son, Charley, was eighteen and away at college. He was a quiet boy, reserved, and had never seen eye to eye with Carlos. Ariana had been somewhat distant throughout his upbringing and had focused mostly on being a good provider while doing well at work. Ariana only thought about the best way to let him know about the divorce and hoped it would not affect him as much as it would if custody were at stake.

Jacqueline made a list of the assets she shared with Phil, then took a stroll to Central Park, where it was unexpectedly quiet. Only a few couples, some with children and some alone, enjoyed the cool evening breeze that helped Jacqueline calm her nerves.

By the time she made it home, Ariana had already gotten ready and was touching up her makeup with a hint of red lipstick.

"Where to?" Jacqueline asked.

"I'm meeting Will for dinner!" said Ariana excitedly.

"Have fun! I wouldn't drink tonight if I were you," scolded Jacqueline. Ariana smirked suggestively and wished her a good night.

Ariana and William met only two blocks away and greeted each other candidly. She looked him up and down with an insipid grin, taking in the crisp, clean scent that she found pleasantly intoxicating.

William and Ariana walked in to find the restaurant unusually busy, but the glowing lights and soft background music set the scene for a romantic evening. Ariana sat down and asked for the wine list.

"The sommelier will be right over, ma'am," replied the hostess warmly and walked away. William asked Ariana whether she would mind letting him choose the wine, and she didn't object.

William was academically accomplished, but his manners seemed stiff and rehearsed, as though he had worked for years at polishing his tastes. To Ariana, whether a man came from money was irrelevant; as long as they dressed well.

William was not a wine connoisseur, but he had made it his business to learn about some good wines for those special occasions when he cared to impress. After surveying the list, he ordered a bottle of Australian red wine. The waiter handed them menus and explained the special for that night: "The paired menu offers small versions of each dish on our menu, each one paired with a wine suggested by our chef," he said.

Ariana was thrilled with the experience, and William liked the idea of trying each gourmet dish on the menu. They both requested the full paired menu and enjoyed an unusually long dinner and intimate talk. Ariana talked mostly about herself, and William laughed at her jokes and mannerisms for most of the evening. Ariana asked William for details about his married life and divorce story, but he avoided the subject, citing his preference to talk about his work. William paid the tab and walked Ariana to Jacqueline's building, ready to call it a night and conscious that they'd both had too much to drink. Unlike Ariana, William was a light drinker and felt lightheaded.

Ariana thanked him for walking with her, but it was not until their farewell embrace that he stumbled and she noticed his tired gaze.

"You shouldn't drive like this," said Ariana. God, you've had way too much to drink. Come upstairs and I'll make you some coffee."

William's car was parked only a few blocks away. He admitted to feeling unusually tired, and since it had just begun to drizzle, he accepted her invitation. She assured him that after a short rest and a little water and coffee he would feel as good as new, and he agreed. When they arrived, it was after eleven o'clock and Jacqueline had already gone to bed. The apartment was silent. Josefina's dog barked and ran toward them excitedly, but Ariana responded with far less enthusiasm. Locking the puppy away in Phil Junior's room, she saw that Josefina had not made it home from class yet. William followed her, zombie-like, to the hallway. She thought it would be best for William to rest in her bed. He agreed, and she left him there. He fell asleep quickly.

A short while later, Ariana returned to the room, closed the door, and sat on a chair next to the closet door. In the near-total darkness, she changed into a T-shirt and removed William's shoes, placing them on the floor at the foot of the bed. She was reluctant to wake him and sat silently on the edge of the bed at his side. Jacqueline had been right that he was secretive, but still, Ariana felt, there was something about him. And though she did not consider him a good-looking man, she had to admit to herself that the mystery that surrounded him had awakened a certain interest within her.

As she watched him sleep, she couldn't resist kissing him lightly on the cheek. Suddenly, he opened his eyes and encircled her with both arms, his lips devouring her passionately. And she followed his lead. Their clothing dropped to the floor piece by piece as they seduced each other with tender caresses. Suddenly, Ariana took charge, if only for a moment. She trembled with anticipation as she returned his kisses with equal fervor, her hand groping for something under her bed. William was oblivious to this distraction until he felt a harsh pull that intensified his erection, filling him with an ecstasy that ended in the strongest, most intense culmination.

Ariana collapsed next to William, and he put his arm around her. They were both panting. She smiled shyly, and he kissed her cheek before regaining his composure enough to gather the pillows against the headboard. When Ariana leaned over to turn on the lamp on the bedside table, he noticed a strange feeling. After looking down, he stared at her, his eyes widening.

"What the hell is this?" he demanded, seeing his manhood trapped in a metal ring.

"Did you like it?"

"Where did this come from?"

Ariana stood, tied on her robe, and sat next to him again, unable to control her shaking hands.

"Don't be scared," she pleaded in a trembling voice. "I wanted to try it. It's just a little toy ring!" she said.

"I didn't ask you to put this thing on me!" he whispered, enraged.

"Don't worry. I'll take it off," she said.

"Have you used it before?"

"It was new! What do you think?" she hissed indignantly.

"Can you get this thing off me?". The pain caused by the ring was intensifying, and the more he tried to remove it, the more his member swelled.

"Wait. I'll take it off," said Ariana and ran to the bathroom. She ransacked the drawers, looking for anything that could help remove the ring, and emerged carrying a small jar of petroleum jelly and a bath towel. Back in the bedroom, she closed the door.

"Let me see," she said as she smeared an abundance of petroleum jelly over the ring, but it was tight around him. Ariana's eyes rose helplessly to his. She didn't know what to say. William was sweating with panic.

"Call the paramedics. I hate to say it . . . Call the paramedics!" he insisted in a quavering voice while he tried in vain to budge the metal ring. The swelling and grip continued to amplify his extreme pain. "It won't come off. Shit!" he growled, his voice thick with agony.

"Let me try," begged Ariana.

"No! Don't do anything else!" he yelled. Just then, they heard someone enter the apartment. Ariana gasped and jumped up from the bed.

"Josefina!" she said.

"Who's Josefina?"

"I'll be right back," she said and dashed out of the room. She ran to the foyer and bumped into Josefina in the middle of the hallway.

"Who's there?" asked Josefina. "I just heard a man's voice."

"Shh, it's my friend Will."

"I could hear him screaming all the way in the elevator!"

Jacqueline was a light sleeper. The noise and William's scream jarred her awake. She approached them in the hallway.

"Ari, what was that?" Jacqueline inquired, still half asleep.

"Wait. Don't come in. Let me explain," Ariana implored them. "We were only trying to have a good time."

"Who?" asked Jacqueline with an inquisitive frown. "Who's in that room?" Ariana took her hand.

"William and me! Shh," she whispered.

"You brought him into my house? Are you nuts? We don't know that guy!"

"We had a few drinks and, well, he couldn't drive, so I made him some coffee—"

"Coffee? In my son's room? You tell him to leave, now!" commanded Jacqueline, infuriated at Ariana's poor judgment.

"Not really," Ariana tried again. "Come here. Let me explain." Josefina and Jacqueline followed her back to the foyer, and Jacqueline while Ariana related the evening's events.

Josefina stared at Ariana, stunned. "You put a ring on his thing?" she repeated, incredulous.

Ariana nodded, and Jacqueline stared, aghast.

"Don't tell me . . ."

Ariana shook her head. "I've tried, but it just won't come off!"

Josefina leaned closer.

"Aren't those things made of rubber? Get a pair of scissors," she whispered. "Just cut it off . . . the ring, I mean."

Ariana shook her head.

"It's not rubber, Josefina . . . It's a metal ring."

"The man is finished business," said Josefina. "He'll be lucky to have one testicle left after tonight."

"Shh!" Ariana gasped. "Don't say that! He can hear you!"

"I ain't scaring him, that ring is! He might sue you, you know?" said Josefina. She went to her room to drop off her backpack and the dog bolted out, excited to see her. Jacqueline opened Ariana's bedroom door.

"What are you doing, Jacky?" asked Ariana.

"I'll see if I can help you get that thing off!"

William lay on the bed with a towel covering him from the waist down.

Jacqueline eyed him with a pained look. "I never thought we'd be this close, William," she said.

"Ariana is deranged. I don't know what the hell she did, but this thing just won't come off!"

"Okay, let's keep calm. Please, don't mind me taking a look," she said, lowering herself onto the bed next to him.

Jacqueline glanced nervously and ran to the hallway.

"We have to call 911!" wait! she said and dug from the room. She dug a pair of pliers out of a toolbox that she kept in the hallway closet. "Here, Josefina, deal with this. Cut the ring off."

"With pliers?"

"Have you ever used a pair of pliers? Cut it off so we can all go back to bed!" Jacqueline ordered in a hysterical tone.

"That's it. I'm calling 911," said Ariana.

In less than fifteen minutes, the reception desk called the apartment. The fire department had arrived before the paramedics, and two men were waiting outside the front door. Josefina let them into the apartment and explained the emergency. The firefighters cringed as Ariana related the issue at hand. William began to wail hysterically, and everyone in the apartment was relieved when the paramedics walked in, rolling a gurney. One of the paramedics assessed William's condition and they all determined that he needed to be rushed to the emergency room.

At this news, Ariana burst into tears. "I swear, Jacky, I won't have a drop of alcohol ever, ever again in my life!"

Jacqueline hugged her as they watched the paramedics take William out on the gurney. For a split second, she wanted to laugh despite her acute awareness that it was far from a laughing matter.

William was pale, consumed with excrutiating pain. Ariana offered to accompany him to the emergency room, but William refused, and Jacqueline confirmed the imprudence of the idea. Josefina gathered William's clothes and shoes into a shopping bag and placed it at the foot of his stretcher while they waited for the elevator.

In the emergency room, the surgeon on duty and a team of nurses attended him. After more than ninety minutes of tedious effort, they finally removed the circular toy. William's member broke free, though the agonizing pain remained.

Chapter 9

Ariana barely slept that night. She was awfully worried and embarrassed about what she had done to poor William, who, unbeknownst to her, had spent the night at the hospital. She tried to call his cell phone, but her calls were routed to voice mail. As each hour passed with no news from him, she feared he'd undergone a surgical procedure. That thought alone made her cringe.

Jacqueline awoke early the next morning feeling rested, her mood pleasant despite what they had all gone through with William the previous night. She floated out of her bedroom at six o'clock and was surprised to find the aroma of fresh coffee and baked goods scenting the apartment at such an early hour. Josefina had been awake since five that morning, anxious to study for her exams, and had taken it upon herself to bake some fresh muffins and cornbread before their morning AA meeting. Jacqueline poured herself a cup of coffee. Josefina put her books away and sat with her at the table. Hearing her friends in the kitchen, Ariana took a brisk shower, threw on a pair of jeans and a large, loose velvet sweater, and joined them for breakfast. Nono lay on the floor, chewing on a beef snack and keeping them company.

"Poor William," said Jacqueline. "I hope he's okay."

"That's what happens when you get fresh and kinky," said Josefina. "He'll have something to think about next time he tries those weird games."

"It was my fault," Ariana said, her face flushing. "I didn't get the impression he's seen anything like that in his life."

Josefina laughed as she spread butter on her freshly baked muffin. "Hmm . . . I don't know," she said. "Men out there can be a little freaky. You never know."

Jacqueline came back from the kitchen with a small pitcher of freshly squeezed orange juice, which she placed in the middle of the table. "Ari, how did you put that on his thingy without him noticing?" she asked, sitting next to her. "No man can be that absentminded."

"Jacqueline, please. What a question!" Josefina opined, rolling her eyes. "I think he knew exactly what she was up to."

"You think so?" asked Ariana, secretly eager to displace some of the blame.

"Of course!" Josefina raved. "You were slipping a metal ring around his penis. It's not like you were pouring holy water on it. Ding-dong!" she concluded with a theatrical gesture.

Jacqueline turned to Ariana with a knowing smile. "I think you bewitched him with your charms."

"And you know I have many."

They all laughed at Ariana's vainglory. When Josefina asked how dinner had gone with William, Ariana confessed that there was something mysterious about him. His conversation the night before had been as deep as a puddle, and he'd shared hardly any details about his life when she asked. Ariana had shown him pictures of her son, Charley, but he'd refused to show her any photos of his children. He claimed to have just bought a new cell phone that he had not yet used to take pictures. Josefina asked whether she had tried to stalk his Facebook page, and Ariana responded that William was not fond of social media. He even took pride in staying as anonymous as possible.

"What did you talk about, then?" asked Jacqueline as she stacked the dirty plates. Ariana shrugged.

"I talked most of the time, you know . . . about my work, my future plans in real estate. Jokes."

Jacqueline laughed. "So basically, you went on a dinner date to perfect your improvised monologue skills?"

"Pretty much," said Ariana. "I think there's something he's not telling me."

"I think there's a lot he's not telling you. But remember, it's only your second or third encounter. He might be the type who likes to take things slow," Jacqueline speculated in his defense.

Ariana nodded. "You're right," she said. "Maybe he just feels it's too early for deeper conversation."

"Well, I think he's married," asserted Josefina.

"He's not cheating. His phone was on the table the entire time. If he were, wouldn't he hide his phone?"

"I don't know what the real story is, but after last night, he probably won't want to see you again," Jacqueline said.

"I'm better off without a guy like Will, anyway. He's too hard to figure out. All this secrecy is giving me a headache."

Josefina nodded. "Yes, ma'am. Fewer dogs, fewer fleas. And about him not hiding his phone? I can tell you that some men have the audacity to talk to their wives right in front of their mistresses. That's how they get away with it. Boldness in plain sight."

"Many professional men keep two cell phones, one for the family and the other for their patients and the rest of the world," Jacqueline agreed.

"Jacky, he doesn't practice. Besides, he's separated."

"I bet he's still married and his wife has no clue they are separated. That's what Johnson did," said Josefina, rising from the table. "But who cares now? At least I got my papers."

Jacqueline rose from the table and changed her tone. "Ari, let this be the last time you bring a man here."

"I know, Jacky. I'm sorry. I had too much to drink," said Ariana. "I only intended to have a glass of wine with dinner, but then they served that amazing meal with the wine pairings. How could I say no?"

"You should take the AA program more seriously," Jacqueline said with genuine worry in her voice. "I can't remember a single one of your drinking episodes without some dire consequences."

Josefina returned from the kitchen with a pitcher of water and set it on the table. She had heard Ariana's complaints and sat down to address them.

"Ariana, no alcoholic ever starts their drinking career with a shot of tequila in the morning," she said calmly.

"What do you mean?"

"Alcoholism is a progressive condition. It starts with one drink once a day, then two a day, and so on until it dawns on you that you're drinking every day at all waking hours. Before you know it, you're completely out of control—"

"I wouldn't do that," Ariana interrupted defensively.

"Not yet," said Jacqueline. "But if you carry on the way you have been, you probably will. You're so bright and happy, Ari. It would be a shame," she said.

"Do you think I'm an alcoholic?" Ariana asked, doubt beginning to crack her confidence.

"If you're not one by now, you're workin' on it," Jacqueline said, repeating her refrain.

Josefina also shared some experiences from her drinking days, before she'd committed herself to the AA program. It was not until Josefina had sat down with a pen and paper to inventory the compromising situations she had put herself in while under the influence of alcohol that she had realized her condition. It never occurred to Ariana to do such a thing, but she had to admit that she couldn't remember a time when she had enjoyed a single glass of wine without drinking the whole bottle. Chaos afterward had been the norm, with only a few calm nights sprinkled in between. Now that she thought of it that way, she realized she did not understand why. Josefina smiled sympathetically.

"What makes a person an alcoholic is their cravings after the first drink. For some reason, our taste buds and brain chemistry always push us to drink compulsively," she explained. Her eyes radiated compassion, and her smile was sincere, without a trace of judgment. Still, Ariana couldn't bring herself to open up completely. A certain fear of reflecting on her past still gripped her. She confessed that she couldn't imagine committing to AA meetings for the rest of her life. Josefina smiled and agreed. She had felt the same way during her early days in recovery.

"Have you heard of the Sinclair Method?" asked Josefina.

Ariana squinted and shook her head. "No. What's that?" The name sounded like a self-help book to her.

"Over three years ago, when I started working for the old man, well . . . back in those days, I still struggled with alcoholism," she said. "It was my second day working for him, and I was two hours late. I stank of rum and I think I had the worst hangover. His daughter was there, waiting for me. That morning, the moment I walked in, I went straight to the bathroom. I was sick to my stomach and puked twice."

"How did the man's daughter let you care for her father in such a condition?" asked Jacqueline. Josefina shook her head.

"She didn't. She told me she had called her daughter's nanny to come cover for me that day. She saw my face. I was desperate and afraid I would lose my job. When she asked me if I was okay, and what had happened, I lied. I told her I had stomach bug."

"And she believed you?" asked Ariana.

"No," said Josefina in a calm tone. "She sat with me on the couch. When the nanny arrived, she told me she was familiar with my type of stomach bug. She had shown up to her job with such bad hangover that she threw up all her margaritas from the night before."

"She knew," realized Jacqueline.

Josefina nodded sheepishly. "Yes. I was so embarrassed that I teared up right in front of her, but she hugged me. She was very kind and said she would give me a chance to keep the job—but only if I promised to get cleaned up. Her boss had given her the same kind of second chance when she discovered her alcoholism, and I guess she found it fair to pay the favor forward."

"Whoa . . . you were lucky," said Ariana.

"Well, that job was a blessing to me in more ways than one," she admitted. "She explained that she had faced the same problem for years and that she'd found a doctor who helped her enormously. She called him right then and there and made an appointment for me. She even paid for the first four consultations and the prescription."

Jacqueline squeezed Josefina's hand warmly.

"How generous of her!"

"Well, she did deduct the cost of the doctor visits from my salary. But I didn't mind. It saved my life."

"What did the doctor give you? I thought alcoholism couldn't be cured . . . or can it?" Jacqueline asked.

"That doctor told me about the Sinclair Method. This method has been around for years and has cured alcoholism over eighty percent of the time in Europe. It involves taking a pill, naltrexone, one hour before having a drink. The medication works by blocking the release of dopamine. Then, after the first or second drink, we just don't crave it anymore. It actually drowned my obsession. I stopped thinking about it after a while, then began going to the meetings. The advantage is that the withdrawals are not so bad. Three months later, I lost all interest in alcohol. It's nothing short of a miracle," she said passionately. Now she went to the AA meetings so that she wouldn't forget her condition and was grateful and glad to help anyone who asked.

Ariana typed the contact information for Josefina's doctor into her cell phone. A Google search turned up hundreds of positive comments and amazing reviews about the Sinclair Method from people who had struggled to control their alcohol consumption.

She found it astonishing that this medication had been approved by the FDA to treat alcoholism, but there was barely any promotion of it.

"I'll call your doctor right away!" Ariana said. "How much is it?"

Jacqueline stood next to her. "Don't worry, Ari. I can help you cover the doctor visit, and you can pay me back as soon as you're back on your feet."

Ariana smiled and thanked her. Jacqueline had done so much for her, far more than Ariana had asked for or expected.

"Go get dressed, Jacky. We have to go to the meeting," said Ariana, clearing the dirty dishes from the table. She set them on the kitchen counter just as Donna arrived.

"Good morning!" Donna called out, full of energy. They all greeted her warmly, and Jacqueline offered her some of the treats Josefina had made for them that morning. Soon, Josefina excused herself to retrieve her backpack, and the three friends headed to their AA meeting.

When the meeting ended, they returned to Jacqueline's apartment, and Josefina dove right back into her studies.

"Josefina! Come quickly!" Ariana yelled from the living room.

"By God, Ari!" Jacqueline scolded her, "Stop screaming. The neighbors don't need to hear any more of what goes on here."

"My feet hurt," said Ariana unapologetically.

"That is the height of laziness." Jacqueline shook her head. Ariana wasn't offended.

Josefina rushed out of her room, and Ariana beamed as she broke the good news.

"My client replied!" Ariana said, showing her the text.

Josefina sat next to her. "Who? The lady from the funeral business?"

Ariana nodded and called the woman while Josefina turned down the television. While the phone rang on the other end, she turned to Josefina.

"Yes. You know, you have to tell her you worked in a funeral home back in your country. She would much prefer people with experience."

"What will she expect me to say?"

"Nothing. Say yes to everything. I'm sure they'll give you basic training."

When Mrs. Collins answered, she told Ariana she would much rather meet Josefina in person to share the details of the job. Josefina wouldn't have to deal with the corpses directly. Upon hearing this, Josefina was eager to start right away. Her work schedule would be discussed once she met with Mrs. Collins, hopefully that very day.

Ariana thanked Mrs. Collins, and Josefina prepared to leave. She could get her interview out of the way that morning and take a couple of hours to familiarize herself with the funeral home.

"All right, now," said Josefina. "I'm leaving! Wish me luck working with the dead!" she concluded, throwing her wool coat over her shoulders.

"Who died?" asked Jacqueline, walking out of her bedroom dressed for her yoga class.

"I got her a job at a funeral home with my client in Queens!" Ariana announced proudly.

Josefina scribbled the address and phone number of the place on a scrap of paper and left.

"Won't you come to yoga with me?" Jacqueline asked Ariana, who was still lying on the couch, gazing at her phone and taking notes.

"No . . . I need to call Josefina's doctor. Maybe he can help me break this bad habit."

"I think you'll be fine," Jacqueline said. "Have you talked to Charley?"

"I called him last night before I went out with Will. He didn't answer."

"How is he handling the divorce?"

"He and Carlos never got along well," said Ariana. "When I mentioned it, he said it was about time. I guess he thinks it's strange that we've lasted so long together."

"Does Charley know about Carlos and your cousin?"

"No, Jacky. News like that has to be broken in person."

"I question whether you should say anything at all. Let him figure it out. Maybe that would be less shocking."

"I don't know how to tell him. I mean, it's one thing to tell your son that you're divorcing. It's something else entirely to tell him you're divorcing because his dad is gay."

"Yes, I know, but that scenario is a lot more common nowadays."

"The fact that it happens all the time now doesn't make it any easier. It's a hard pill to swallow."

Jacqueline hugged her. "I'm here to support you any way I can."

"Thanks, Jacky. These issues are too sensitive. I think I owe it to Charley to explain it to him in private. In fact, can you pretend to know nothing about it?"

Jacqueline nodded and changed the subject, asking whether Ariana had heard anything from William. Ariana had tried calling a few times but suspected his phone was dead, because she could only reach his voice mail. Perhaps the man had blocked her number; Jacqueline would be surprised if he hadn't. His encounters with Ariana had been undeniably memorable for all the wrong reasons. However, Ariana was not sensitive about William's disappearing act. After all, he was not her type. Although she admitted to Jacqueline that she found him fascinating, she wasn't genuinely attracted to him and admitted that perhaps he was only a placeholder, a warm body to amuse her during her painful separation.

Chapter 10

Josefina left Jacqueline's apartment and made her way to the funeral home, unsure of what to expect. During her commute, she changed trains several times, ignoring the bustle around her. She walked briskly through the platform of each subway station until she finally made it to Queens. Her confidence drooped when she realized her destination was in a fairly secluded area and she'd have to take a bus that made more than a few stops. Her stop was four blocks from the funeral home. The trip had taken longer than expected. Josefina was not yet employed, but she already resented the tedious trek she would have to make to get to her job.

She approached the front of the building, scanning her surroundings and checking the scrap of paper she'd retrieved from her pocket. She had the right address.

The funeral home was a grand Victorian-style house with a renovated facade. She could smell fresh paint. Above the entrance was a sign with golden letters: "Collins Brothers' Funeral Home."

Josefina walked into the lobby, which reminded her of a private school. She bumped into a lady who looked at her with broad eyes and a candid smile that accentuated her chubby pink cheeks. Her manners clearly conveyed her simplicity.

"Hello! Good afternoon," said the lady with a shrill voice. She greeted Josefina with the enthusiasm of a host at a birthday party.

"My name is Josefina. I'm Ariana's friend from the city. She called you earlier today?" Josefina said timidly.

"Hello, Josefina. Yes! What a pleasure to meet you. Come to my office. I'm the owner, Lisa Collins."

Josefina followed her, taking in her surroundings. She found it welcoming and well furnished, with a cozy atmosphere despite its purpose. It was the opposite of the experience in her village years ago, the goose bump-inducing vigil that had so repelled her.

"Do you always play this kind of music, ma'am?" Josefina asked.

"Yes. It helps us to maintain the formality of the occasion," said Mrs. Collins. "Ariana told me you have experience working in morgues and funeral homes. Is that correct?"

Josefina's hands felt sweaty, and she wasn't sure whether to attribute her newly acquired set of nerves to the question or the place.

"Yes, but the funerals in my hometown in the Dominican Republic are probably different from the ones here," said Josefina in a choked voice, clearing her throat before she continued. "My town is small and they may use different methods."

She was already looking for excuses in case Mrs. Collins realized she had no experience at all working with the dead.

"It doesn't matter," said Mrs. Collins. "We have to train you anyway. First, I want you to fill out the application; it's standard procedure. We need your information on file. Then I'll take you over to meet Manny and Violet so you can get a feel for the place. Manny is the best. He embalms the bodies, and Violet is the aesthetician. She makes sure the corpses look presentable for the wake."

"Aesthetician?" asked Josefina.

"Yes. Only an experienced aesthetician with a special license can work on the bodies, to make them presentable," explained Mrs. Collins as they entered her office.

Josefina felt the undeniable coldness of the place and began to regret her decision to work there.

Mrs. Collins sat behind her desk and handed Josefina a job application that Josefina managed to fill out despite her apprehension. In the work experience section, she wrote of experience she didn't have, in companies that didn't exist.

Josefina was not too concerned. She was certain the old man's daughter would give her an excellent reference if Mrs. Collins decided to ask for one.

Mrs. Collins looked at the document. She read it carefully with an air of doubt, frowning.

"I see that you worked in two funeral homes in Santo Domingo, but there are no phone numbers."

Josefina shrugged.

"One of the funeral homes burned and the other one went out of business two years ago," she said in a resolute tone. "In any case, none of the managers there spoke English. Calling them wouldn't help."

"References are very important to us," said Mrs. Collins. "I assume your documentation is up to date. Are you a US citizen?"

"Yes," said Josefina as she opened her bag and pulled out her wallet. She placed her Social Security card on the desk with a triumphant smile. "I became a citizen four years ago. For references, you can call Mrs. Goldberg. Her phone number is right here," said Josefina, pointing at the application.

"Who's Mrs. Goldberg?"

"I worked for her and her family for more than two years, ma'am. I took care of her father," said Josefina.

"And why did you leave the job?"

"Because the man died a few days ago," Josefina said. "He was very old."

"I see. I want you to walk through the building and see how we operate today. I want you to determine whether you'll be comfortable here or not—just to make sure. Is that all right?" she asked in a compassionate tone.

Josefina nodded, smiling.

They left the office and Mrs. Collins walked straight to a hall closet, where she removed a white coat from its hanger and handed it to Josefina.

"Put this on over your clothes," she said. Josefina followed her instructions with trembling hands.

Mrs. Collins walked to the end of the corridor. Josefina accompanied her into a cold room resembling a hospital kitchen. The walls were covered in ordinary white tiles and lined with stainless steel appliances that were unfamiliar to Josefina.

"This is where they embalm the dead," said Mrs. Collins matter-of-factly.

Josefina watched stiffly from the doorway as a man with Asian features sewed an incision in the corpse's wrist with a kind of thick white thread.

"Hi!" He looked up at Josefina, and Mrs. Collins signaled her to come closer.

"Come. This is Manny." She nodded toward the Asian man. Josefina could feel the color draining from her face, but she had seen dead bodies more than a few times at vigils back home. Though the scenery turned her stomach, she felt strong enough to endure at least a few hours of work there without fainting. Manny's assistant was a thin redheaded young man with a generous splatter of freckles. He looked up and smiled at Josefina while she watched Manny remove a long transparent tube that protruded from the corpse's ankle. It was apparently inserted through an incision and used to drain the blood from the body.

Manny closed that last incision, walked to a stainless steel cabinet, and pulled out a mask. He handed it to Josefina, and the redheaded assistant helped her adjust it on her face.

"Keep it on," said Manny. "It helps to filter the air."

"The corpses give off a peculiar smell," said Mrs. Collins, hooking her own mask over her ears.

Josefina immediately felt a swirl of knots in the pit of her stomach and found herself yearning for the familiar drudgery of cleaning restaurant kitchens.

Manny grabbed a hose with a shower head and rinsed the body of the dead girl on the flat metal gurney. She seemed young, in her late twenties or early thirties. His assistant applied a pink liquid soap gently, as though he were bathing a delicate doll. The soap was a disinfectant gel with a special pink pigment designed to disguise the yellow and grayish skin of dead bodies and tame the powerful odor of decomposition.

Manny's assistant dried the body and covered it with a white sheet. Manny showed Josefina what products to use in case she took the job and was expected to help bathe corpses.

Josefina and Mrs. Collins followed the men to the next room, where they prepped the bodies for the wake. The room's walls were lined with shelves. Josefina was amazed to see so many shelves overflowing with personal care items and different kinds of makeup.

Violet, the beautician, greeted Josefina with an absent gaze that was not easy to decipher. She was a thin young woman with long legs and a long neck and a hump that spoiled her otherwise elegant figure. Her velvety face looked chalk-white and contrasted sharply with the jet-black hair she kept in a prim ponytail, shining like glass.

Violet dressed the cadaver while Mrs. Collins shared about the most difficult part of the business—she knew the aunt of the deceased girl.

Mrs. Collins spoke and Josefina listened as Violet finished dressing the corpse. The young woman had died in a car crash while driving from Manhattan to Queens. Her boyfriend had also died in the crash.

The girl's aunt had told Mrs. Collins that the girl was driving to a surprise party the family had prepared for her mother. It was her mother's fifty-fifth birthday.

The boyfriend's body was so shattered by the impact that his family preferred to cremate him. "I met her twice," said Mrs. Collins. "This work has a way of desensitizing people."

"What was her name?" asked Josefina, feeling a disturbing curiosity. She couldn't explain her compulsion to ask this question.

"Her name was Reyna," said Mrs. Collins, helping Violet fasten the buttons on the back of the dress.

"That's an unusual Spanish name for an American girl. It means 'queen' in Spanish," she mumbled timidly, a lump rising in her throat. She watched as Manny massaged the girl's hands and Violet finished her makeup.

Mrs. Collins looked up at Josefina's pale face and wide eyes.

"Watch and learn," she said. "Soon you'll be helping Violet dress them, too."

Josefina nodded without smiling and turned her attention to Violet, who was now sharing about some crazy experience she'd had on her last trip to Colorado.

Violet finished dressing the young woman and carefully retouched every detail of her makeup.

Despite dying from a severe impact with a cargo truck, the girl's face wasn't disfigured. The windshield had only managed to inflict a circular bruise that stained her face with a blue shadow from the tip of her chin to the center of her forehead.

Manny and Violet rolled the gurney to the chapel, which resembled a formal living room. Josefina followed, carrying the makeup bag.

In the chapel, Josefina walked alongside Manny and Violet, placed the makeup bag on the floor, and helped Manny move the body from the stretcher to the coffin. The coffin was beautifully crafted from mahogany, its interior lined with fine white sheets.

Violet spread a large white cotton bib over the young woman's torso and finished the last details of the makeup. After dusting off her hands, she applied a rosy lip gloss to the dead girl's lips and arranged the corpse's hair into perfect curls with the help of a curling iron. Manny attached the corpse's feet together with a thick metal safety pin.

Josefina followed Violet back to the makeup room and helped her clean up. When they were finished, Josefina took off her white coat and handed it to Mrs. Collins. The flower arrangements were beginning to arrive.

Manny and Mrs. Collins positioned the flowers in front of the coffin, tributes to the girl who slept eternally, who was the focus of much grief that day but would live on in many loving memories.

Josefina was now convinced that regardless of need, she could never work in a funeral home. She shared her regret with Mrs. Collins plainly, admitting that the work would better suit a more practical person and she did not fit that description. Mrs. Collins expressed sympathetic appreciation for her honesty and escorted her gently to the front door.

Josefina walked out of the place feeling like a sack of wet sand, her nerves on edge and her mind clouded. Luckily for her, within a week she'd be finished with school and would hopefully find a good job soon.

That afternoon, Jacqueline met with Jeff in his office and talked about the list she had emailed him the day before. Jacqueline and Phil owned numerous properties, but she only cared to keep her apartment and a property they owned in South Florida. She had no interest in maintaining the numerous assets and real estate. To her, hard cash and a good alimony would be the most convenient and reasonable solution.

Jeff agreed with her, and since she was his last client, he invited her to dinner and she gladly accepted. Ariana had called during their meeting, and Jeff encouraged Jacqueline to invite her as well. They met Ariana at an Italian restaurant near Jacqueline's apartment. The place seemed uncharacteristically quiet, but the good food and tranquility offered a calming end to a busy workday, for Jeff, anyway.

"Do you think Phil will complain about what I'm asking for?" Jacqueline inquired.

Jeff smiled. "I don't know. You have enough reason to accept no less," he said in a low voice. "Phil didn't even have a house when he married you. Thanks to your father and then your inheritance, you guys paid off the mortgage on the apartment. It's paid off, right?" Jacqueline shook her head. "No. I mean, it was. He took out a mortgage on it last year."

"And why did you sign that? Are you crazy?" said Ariana.

"What was I supposed to do?" Jacqueline lamented, feeling cornered. "Phil said he had to cover some other expenses and that we were behind on mortgage payments for the house in the Hamptons."

"And that house?" Jeff asked. "Is it up to date?"

"Yes. After we mortgaged the apartment, Phil told me he'd paid it up, so I stopped worrying. It's been on the market for a year now. As far as I know, it hasn't sold."

"I think that bastard has been planning to divorce you for quite some time. That's why he took out the mortgage on your apartment," Ariana said, dipping her spoon in the tiramisu on the plate they shared in the center of the table.

"Maybe," Jeff said. "I think your demands are pretty reasonable. But tomorrow I'll make a couple of adjustments to your proposal. We want to make sure you're not taking on any debt."

"The least he can do is be a decent person and let me and the boys keep the apartment and give me a decent alimony," Jacqueline said.

"I didn't tell you this, but Phil and I had a meeting scheduled for this morning. He missed it," Jeff said.

"What meeting?" Jacqueline's eyes narrowed.

"We had arranged to meet earlier today. I wanted to see his offer before I spoke with you," said Jeff.

"And what did he tell you?" Jacqueline asked, her voice rising in suspense.

"He didn't show and never called to cancel, either. His lawyer called and said Phil was going through a tough time right now. I don't know what happened, but I'll speak with him tomorrow."

"Do you think I should call him?" Jacqueline said.

"No," said Jeff. "I'll let you know what's going on, but it sounds like he's in bad shape. I'll know more tomorrow."

"How are you gonna call him? He has a restraining order against you!" Ariana said. "He can go to hell!"

"If it had something to do with the children, you would've told me, right?" said Jacqueline.

"Of course. It doesn't involve them. We'll know tomorrow," Jeff concluded, not wanting to give weight to the matter.

"Don't worry about it, Jacky," Ariana said. "Look what he did to you! He cheated and dumped you! Asshole!"

"He's the father of my children, Ari," said Jacqueline with unusual calm. "If something happens to him, my boys will also suffer. And now let's talk about something else. Not another word."

Jeff paid the bill and walked with Ariana and Jacqueline to their building at Fifty-Sixth Street and Fifth Avenue. He raised his hand to signal a vacant taxi. The cab squealed to a stop right in front of the building.

Ariana and Jacqueline said goodbye with a hug and thanked him for dinner, then stood on the sidewalk watching as the cab drove away. Jacqueline's stomach churned at the thought of Phil tricking her out of her finances. She was, however, concerned about his well-being and hoped his problems were not health-related. He was, after all, the father of her kids, and although she wanted to divorce him, she wished him well.

Jacqueline and Ariana arrived upstairs quietly. Jacqueline felt relieved knowing that the next day the restraining order would be lifted and she could finally see her boys. She missed them so much. She was eager to gauge their mental state after everything Phil had put them through.

That same night, Ariana called her son, Charley, more than six times, but her calls went unanswered. After leaving several messages, she lay in bed thinking about the distant relationship she now realized she had with her son. Charley had always been reserved, she said to herself. She remembered his childhood with a broad smile. She had always worked hard to ensure that her son never wanted for the basics, and knowing she'd been an amazing provider made her proud. Her mind traveled to some of their more bitter moments, when her boy was young and mischievous, throwing tantrums toward his nanny.

In those days, Ariana had been young and more inclined toward work and fun. She often bought her freedom by giving extravagant gifts to those who cared for her son in her absence. Her conscience shook her now, ruffling her emotions with vivid memories that forced her to admit to herself that she had been an absentee mother. Her newly acquired sobriety had finally enlightened her, changing her perception of life, her past shortcomings, and herself. She had not been the great mother she thought she was, and realizing this made her soul feel naked with pain.

Ariana drowned in her internal struggle, managing to absorb a humbling lesson. Her guilt was inevitable, but it was a small price to pay to get her life back, and she hoped to make up for lost time with Charley. She hugged her pillow and burst into tears before falling asleep.

Josefina arrived at midnight, exhausted from her foray into the funeral business and her effort at passing her first exam. Despite her poor English language skills, she managed to score the third highest grade of the entire class. Josefina's path, like Ariana's, was beginning to take shape. She needed only to pass four more exams, and then she'd be able to work as a medical assistant and turn her life around.

Divorcing Johnson would be her next biggest accomplishment, but she was in no hurry. She had no assets or children to fight for.

Josefina cleaned the area where she kept Nono during the day and washed up before lying down for the night. She was now more grateful than ever, knowing she was only a few steps from a better paying job.

Dealing with her problems one step at a time and living her life one day at a time had almost miraculously paved her way to a better life.

Chapter 11

Ariana had finally come to terms with her recreational drinking style and felt the urge to share a few anecdotes at the AA meeting the next morning. She described the chaos that had characterized most of her adult life, admitting openly for the first time that once she started drinking, she couldn't stop.

Josefina had gone through that same struggle years before and understood firsthand how difficult it was to acknowledge she had a problem. Luckily, Ariana wasn't alone, and after the meeting a few of the members approached her to offer much-needed support.

Josefina nudged Ariana with a knowing smile. "Maybe now the AA meetings will make more sense to you."

"I feel as though a huge weight has been lifted off my shoulders." said Ariana as the three of them walked out of the building. "I've already scheduled an appointment with the doctor you recommended."

"You won't regret seeing him. I'm so glad I did," said Josefina. "He's a little weird, but he really is amazing."

"Most brilliant people are a little weird," Jacqueline thought aloud. "He's probably a Nobel Prize winner in the making if he can cure alcoholism."

Ariana wanted to know her sober self. She admitted she needed to learn how to conquer her fears, problems, and anxieties without depending on mind-altering substances. Jacqueline's support provided the normalcy she'd need to rediscover herself during her time of crisis.

That afternoon, Josefina met with the daughter of the old man she used to care for. She had called Josefina early that morning and asked her to meet at the old man's apartment to pick up some things she had left behind while working there. Josefina hoped his daughter would refer her to a new job.

When Jacqueline and Ariana arrived at the apartment, Jacqueline went to her room to change into something more comfortable, while Ariana helped Donna fold and sort the clean laundry. Before they finished, Ariana's cell phone rang, but by the time she was able to dig it out of her purse, the call had gone to voice mail.

"Who was it?" Jacqueline asked as she lifted her purse from the table in the foyer.

Ariana listened anxiously to the message. "It's my friend, the banker!"

"What did he say?"

"Nothing, really. Just to call him back."

"I hope you can get that job in the office complex."

Ariana smiled and nodded. "Me too," she said and retired to her room to return the call.

Jacqueline was on the way out for a much-anticipated walk in Central Park when Jeff called. "Hello?"

"It's Jeff. Can you talk?"

"Of course. What's going on?" Jacqueline put her purse down and sat on the sofa.

"Phil didn't come to the meeting today, either," he said.

"What happened? Is he okay?"

"I don't know. His lawyer said that he's having a hard time but didn't explain why."

"What do you think might have happened?" Jacqueline fretted. "Are my children okay?"

"Yes, your boys are fine. I just don't know what's going on with Phil. We should know something soon. In the meantime, stay calm. Maybe

Phil will stop by the office sometime later," said Jeff soothingly. "You know how moody he can be."

"I'm not so sure 'moody' is the right word. I think 'obnoxious' is a more accurate term," snorted Jacqueline.

"His lawyer said he would speak to him, but Phil is not answering his calls today."

"When will I see the boys?"

"As soon as Phil brings them to the office, as agreed. If he doesn't come then, he'll send them to your place. I'll keep you informed," Jeff said resolutely. His calmness was contagious, and the mere act of talking to him infused Jacqueline with invaluable serenity.

Jeff explained that after she completed the ninety-day AA program, she would no longer be required to go. They both knew Jacqueline's problems had nothing to do with alcohol consumption and everything to do with Phil's abuse and manipulation.

Jacqueline was about to hang up when Jeff got a call from Phil's attorney. Jeff told Jacqueline he'd call her back when he knew exactly what was happening with Phil. After a few minutes, he called back and revealed that Phil's lawyer seemed more complaisant than usual but was unwilling to discuss Phil's whereabouts.

That evening, Phil didn't show up at Jeff's office and instead arranged transportation for the boys. A chauffeur would be dropping them off at Jacqueline's apartment within a couple of hours. Jeff also informed Jacqueline that she and Phil would share custody until they hammered out a custody agreement once the divorce was finalized.

"Did you ask him about Phil?" Jacqueline probed.

"Yes," said Jeff, "but he said he wouldn't share any details about Phil's situation until tomorrow. He sounded like he was in a hurry to get off the phone."

"What time are they dropping off my kids?"

"At seven, I think. I'll call you when they're on the way."

Jacqueline thanked him for his dedication and good work. Before hanging up, they agreed to call each other if either of them heard anything about Phil's situation or whereabouts. As Jacqueline hung up, she noticed that Donna, who had been listening to her side of the conversation, was visibly ecstatic.

"The boys will come home today?" Donna asked.

Jacqueline nodded, her eyes brimming with jubilant tears. Donna hugged her.

"Soon this nightmare will be over," said Donna happily. "Let's go get some groceries!"

At the supermark, they shopped for staples, but popcorn, chocolate bars, and a few sugary snacks also found their way into the shopping cart.

Ariana had finished her phone call and was relaxing on the sofa when they returned. Jacqueline shared her news about the boys, and while another time Ariana would have celebrated their return with a bottle of champagne, this time she was content to celebrate with a warm hug and a cold glass of ginger tea.

"Did you speak to your banker friend?" Jacqueline asked, arranging the groceries in the pantry.

"Yes. He gave me both good news and bad news," Ariana said.

"What do you mean?"

"Well," said Ariana, "his partner has an apartment building in New Jersey they want to convert into condominiums for sale."

"And what does he want you to do? Sell that project instead?" Jacqueline guessed, pouring herself a glass of iced tea.

"The point is that there's a couple who . . . well, the husband owns a large share in that building. The other investors want to turn it into a condo conversion, and he's holding out."

"And what does he want you to do?"

"My friend bragged to his partners about what a great salesperson I am. To make a long story short, he wants me to meet with that couple and hopefully convince the husband to agree to convert the rentals to condos. My friend said his partner would be willing to make me a sales manager for one of their new projects, a condominium building in Soho. We'd be selling the units at preconstruction prices. But my friend told me that if I can get this guy to change his mind, the job will be almost guaranteed."

"So that's the catch," said Jacqueline, unimpressed.

"Yes, of course, Jacky. Nothing worthwhile comes easily. They'll be selling the units at preconstruction prices next month!"

"You'll earn a fortune!" said Jacqueline, genuinely happy for her.

"Yes, ma'am . . . but I have to win over that couple. Hopefully I can sell the husband on the idea of a condo conversion," Ariana said. She finished her ice tea and grabbed her bag.

"Where are you going?" Donna asked.

"I have a doctor's appointment. I'm already late! His office is open to new patients until eight today." Ariana opened the door and stepped into the hallway, but Jacqueline rushed after her.

"I forgot to tell you that you'll be sharing your room with Josefina tonight. The kids will be home shortly."

"I know. You told me an hour ago. Will Phil Junior be sharing his room with Mark, then?"

Jacqueline nodded. "Yes. Tonight, we'll talk about the best way to help Josefina until she finishes her exams."

"If I do well tomorrow—with that couple, I mean—maybe my friend can give me an advance to get myself a studio until I get my share of the money from the house."

"That would be ideal," said Jacqueline.

Ariana nodded. "Yes. I love being here with you, but I really feel like I need my own space."

"I'm sure we'll work it out. Here!" Jacqueline handed her an envelope.

"What's this?"

"That's Will's ambulance bill. I'm not paying for that, you know."

"I'll take care of it as soon as I get a hold of him. He seems to have vanished from the face of the earth!" said Ariana, walking toward the elevator.

Jacqueline wished her good luck at her doctor's appointment and walked back inside to help Donna clean the boys' room. They gathered Josefina's possessions and moved Nono from the room. Donna made an effort to place all her clothes on the bed as neatly as possible.

"Where should we put them?" Donna asked, seeing that Ariana had taken the little space left in the closet and the only empty drawer in that room.

"Wait here. I'll be right back," Jacqueline said. She fetched a medium-sized navy blue suitcase from the top of her closet.

"The poor thing," Jacqueline murmured, opening the suitcase and laying it on the floor. "Put this sheet in the laundry. I'll arrange everything in this suitcase."

"Are you giving it to her to keep?"

"Yes. Why not?"

Jacqueline organized Josefina's clothes and left the suitcase unzipped but closed it to keep Nono from making a mess of her things. Soon, Josefina arrived at the apartment in a much more cheerful mood than when she had left.

"How was your old boss?" Jacqueline asked.

"Very well." She took Jacqueline's hand. "Thank you so much for helping me."

Jacqueline hugged her. Something about that moment gave her the impression Josefina wouldn't need to stay with her much longer.

"You've done so much for us, too, Josefina. Look at Ariana! I was afraid that getting her to see her drinking problem was a lost cause, but now she's meeting with your doctor."

"If she follows his instructions, she'll do great," Josefina said.

"So how did it go with the old man's daughter?" asked Jacqueline on her way to the kitchen.

Josefina followed. "I have a new job!" she said excitedly.

"Where?"

"The old man's daughter has a brother-in-law who's very sick. He had a stroke a while ago."

"Oh!"

"The family needs someone to take care of him, and his old nurse went back to Detroit with her husband. His job transferred him. They'll pay me two thousand dollars a month, and since I'll be sleeping there, I can save money on rent."

"That sounds like a great job for you right now! You'll be able to save some money and get your life back in order," Jacqueline said. She was overjoyed for her. "Where does the brother-in-law live?"

"Near the Catskills, about an hour from here."

"I imagine that in a suburban area like that, you might need a car to get around," said Jacqueline.

"I have my own driver! Uber!" she quipped, and they both laughed.

"True. I'm sure you'll love it over there. What's happening with your divorce?" Jacqueline asked.

"I still need to find a lawyer. I can't afford one now, but I'll make it happen as soon as I get my first paycheck," Josefina said. She wasn't worried.

Josefina expected to finish her exams on Monday and planned to move out on Tuesday. Jacqueline reassured her that she was in no hurry for her to leave, but Josefina insisted. She wanted to start her new job as soon as possible. Jacqueline led her to Mark's room, where Ariana had been staying.

"Look, Josefina," she said, pointing at the suitcase on the floor. "I hope you don't mind. Donna and I took it upon ourselves to fold your clean laundry. The sheet you bundled everything in was very dirty. It's in the dryer now. My children arrive today, and since both rooms have a sofa bed, I didn't think you'd mind bunking with Ariana. The boys will stay in the other room until we get everything sorted out."

Josefina crouched in front of the neatly organized suitcase and grinned up at Jacqueline. "Thanks! I needed a suitcase!" she said gratefully, and Jacqueline laughed.

"We already knew that," she said. "That's why I gave you that one. I haven't used it in years. It's all yours."

Although she had no intention of pressuring her to move out, Jacqueline was relieved to learn that Josefina would be leaving in a couple of days. As long as Ariana was successful at her upcoming appointment with the couple, everything would be in place for Jacqueline to breathe in the sweet scent of normalcy again.

Josefina bathed her dog with Jacqueline's help. Jacqueline had taken a liking to the puppy and knew that her boys would adore him as well. The boys had always wanted a pet, but Phil refused to allow it. Earlier that day, at the supermarket, Jacqueline had bought Josefina a bottle of dog shampoo, a few toys, and some puppy treats.

Donna whipped up some macaroni and cheese and sweet and sour chicken fingers, the boys' favorite. At about seven o'clock, Jeff called. Phil was apparently dealing with a personal problem. Someone close to him had died and he was an emotional wreck, according to his attorney, which prevented him from meeting at Jeff's office. The children had eaten dinner with their father and were now on the way. They would be arriving around seven thirty that evening.

Since the boys had already been fed, Jacqueline served the chicken and the macaroni and cheese and complemented the colorful meal with a delicious salad. Ariana arrived at the apartment within a few minutes, and Jacqueline invited her and Josefina to join her at the dinner table. Josefina joined her, while Donna excused herself.

"I can't, Jacky," said Donna. "My husband left his keys back at work, and he's waiting for me at the station."

Jacqueline thanked her for helping her organize Josefina's belongings, and Donna moved Josefina's dog to Phil Junior's bedroom and closed the door before using the bathroom. Shortly after, she left.

Jacqueline and Josefina sat at the dining table, engaging in conversation.

"I wonder who in Phil's world passed away. He's acting so strange," Jacqueline said.

"Who?" asked Ariana.

"Phil. Jeff told me someone close to him died."

Josefina took a sip of water, and her eyes grew large. "Wanna hear something horrific?" asked Josefina secretively.

"Not really . . ." said Jacqueline, smiling coyly.

"I do!" said Ariana in her usual shameless manner, helping herself to a small portion of salad.

"Yesterday, when I went to work at your friend's funeral home, the service was for a young girl—so pretty, and so young!" Josefina said, remembering the girl in the coffin.

"Do you know what happened to her?" Jacqueline asked.

"She died in a car crash. Her boyfriend also died, but he was in such bad shape, the family chose to cremate him."

"How do you know the details?" asked Ariana.

"Your friend, Mrs. Collins, told me. She knew the girl's family. Her name was Reyna. Isn't that an unusual name for an American girl?" Josefina mused, chewing a bite of chicken. "It means 'queen' in Spanish."

Jacqueline and Ariana's eyes met, and their jaws dropped.

"Reyna?" Jacqueline repeated with her mouth hanging open.

"Yes . . . what?"

"Wait," spat Ariana, and she rushed to the foyer to get her purse. She found her cell phone and sat back down at the table. "I'm checking her Facebook page," she said, and Jacqueline leaned over her shoulder.

"It can't be the same girl," said Jacqueline.

"No. That would be too much of a coincidence," Ariana agreed.

A moment later, Ariana passed the phone to Jacqueline. Jacqueline flipped through the girl's profile, her face tense and her heart pounding vigorously. She wiped her hands and xhaled heavily.

"I can't believe it. This cannot be happening . . . It's impossible . . ." she said in a strained voice.

Stunned, Ariana stared as Jacqueline ran to her bedroom and slammed the door. Josefina and Ariana got up from the table and ran to check on her.

"What happened?" Josefina asked Ariana.

"I'll explain it in a minute," she replied, stepping into Jacqueline's bedroom. Jacqueline was sitting on the side of her bed, making a call.

"Hi, Jeff . . . do you know if Phil's girlfriend had a car accident?" asked Jacqueline, her hands shaking and heart pounding violently.

"What? Who said that?" he asked.

"Reyna. Is she the one close to Phil who passed away?" She turned to Ariana. "What was her last name?" she yelled frantically.

Ariana flipped through her phone's history to find the girl's profile again.

"Reyna Agosti!" she reported.

Jacqueline repeated the name to Jeff. He was silent. "Jeff! Are you there?"

"Yes. Yes . . ." he said finally. "That's her last name, all right . . ."

"That's why Phil's been acting so strange!" said Jacqueline. "Please find out if his girlfriend is the one who died," she insisted, near hysteria.

"Karma is a bitch," Ariana whispered.

"Don't call Phil," Jeff advised. "I'll call his lawyer in the morning and let you know what I find out. Don't call him or talk to anyone else about it."

After agreeing to comply with these instructions, Jacqueline lowered the phone with trembling hands and a pale face. "I can't believe it," she said again.

Josefina interrupted them. "Your husband's girlfriend? I don't think it's the same person. The dead girl seemed too young to me. Besides, her boyfriend was in the car with her when she died."

"Phil isn't dead," said Ariana flatly.

"Of course he's not dead! He spoke to his lawyer earlier today, just this morning!" Jacqueline retorted, ripping her sweater off and throwing it on the bed.

"Surely it must have been another Reyna," Josefina said. "That would be a hell of a coincidence."

Jacqueline looked up at Josefina. "How do you know she was with her boyfriend?"

"Because Mrs. Collins is friends with the girl's aunt. The boyfriend's family opted to cremate him because he was crushed in the wreck—or at least that's what she told me . . ."

Jacqueline rose from the bed with chills and went into the bathroom to turn on the shower. "Then, most likely, we're talking about someone else," she concluded.

Josefina and Ariana left the room and finished dinner while Jacqueline drowned her anxiety in a hot bath.

"Between you and me," said Ariana, "I don't think there are two Reyna Agostis. That's not a common name!"

"She seemed much too young to date a fifty-something-year-old man," said Josefina.

Ariana rolled her eyes and glanced at her. "Oh, please. When has age ever stopped a gold digger from latching on to a rich man?"

Josefina shrugged, and they put away the leftovers. By the time they finished wiping the table and the kitchen counters, Jacqueline had emerged from her bedroom with a more pleasant demeanor. Soon, her boys arrived, and she hugged them both with tears of joy.

The apartment door was standing open, and one suitcase sat on the floor. Randy stood next to it, his face haggard. Jacqueline stared at him, suddenly aware that his presence embittered the joyous moment.

She walked briskly to the door and snatched the suitcase from his side. Her face had transformed instantaneously to an expression of rage, and he noticed.

"Ma'am, are you all right?" he asked.

"What the hell do you care?" she hissed. "Get out of my house, and the next time you have to come pick up or drop off my children, stay outside my property where you belong! Now go back to Phil's side ass and get the hell out of my sight, you two-faced good-for-nothing."

Even Jacqueline was surprised at her tone. At the same time, she couldn't overlook Randy's disloyalty. He had covered for Phil's escapades and helped him take her kids away while stabbing her in the back and causing her to question her own self-worth. Not knowing how to face her or what to say, he turned around and left.

Ariana smiled proudly. In her short time outside the grip of Phil's abuse, Jacqueline had changed. She'd learned how to stand up for herself and was no longer the insecure, complacent woman she had been only a month before. Phil's absence had served her well.

Mark wouldn't let go of Jacqueline. He hugged her again and again, almost as if he were trying to convince himself she was really there. He stood, gripping her arm, as he watched Phil Junior drag his suitcase to his room.

"Finally, I get to sleep in my own bed," Phil Junior sighed.

"You have to share the room with your brother, just for the next few days," Jacqueline said and closed the apartment door.

"But, Mom!" the boy protested.

"I don't want any complaints! Auntie Ari is staying with us for a few days and I'm not about to make her sleep in the living room," Jacqueline said, ruffling Mark's hair affectionately.

Phil Junior nodded. The moment the boy opened his bedroom door, his face lit up. Nono was equally happy to see a new playmate. He erupted into a frenzy of jumping and barking, then ran to the foyer, where Mark released Jacqueline's captive arm to pet him. Both boys were now jumping for joy at the unexpected surprise.

"A puppy!" Mark shrieked, throwing his backpack to the floor. Nono ran in circles, then jumped on his new friend, licking his face.

"Whose is he?" Phil Junior asked.

"He's Josefina's," said Jacqueline, gesturing toward her friend, who was sitting in the living room.

That night, Jacqueline forbade them to talk about their father or the divorce. Those were grown-up issues, and she would sit with them and tell them what they needed to know in due time. She asked how they had spent their time that month and how they were doing in school, and little Mark surprised her with news of improvement in all his grades. He had not forgotten her promise of horseback riding lessons and was eager for summer to arrive so he could start in that exciting sport.

"Okay," Jacqueline said. "But you have to keep those good grades up. I'm so proud of you."

They all went to bed late that night after watching a couple movies together. Josefina's dog never left Mark's side. Ariana couldn't help noticing the boys' attachment to their mother, and for a moment she felt envious. The evening had been so cozy and delightful that it made her realize how much joy there was in sober living. She was determined to win her son's affection and respect. Together, they would surely make up for lost time.

Chapter 12

The next morning, Jacqueline left the children with Donna and walked to the AA meeting as usual with Ariana and Josefina. Back at home afterward, Ariana changed into a business suit.

"Where are you going?" Jacqueline asked playfully while writing notes in her datebook.

"Jersey. I have to meet that couple at the apartment building," Ariana replied. "Wish me luck! I need to persuade them to sign off on the condo conversion."

"And what if they don't sign it?" Jacqueline inquired.

"I'll figure something out. I can't worry about that right now. Gotta stay focused."

"If signing that agreement means you'll be getting the job downtown, I'd take a gun with me if I were you!" Jacqueline joked.

"That's not a bad idea," Ariana played along. "But I bet I can get them to change their minds with my expert sales skills." She struck a pose as she walked out of the apartment.

Jacqueline took her boys shopping at the electronics store. She was looking for a new laptop, thinking she might take computer classes and catch up with the online world. Phil Junior perused the popular video games while Mark tested an iPad.

With their decisions made, they stood in line to pay for their purchases. "Mommy, can we get pizza?" Mark asked.

"But we just had breakfast," Jacqueline said, handing her credit card to the cashier. "We need to get you a new pair of sneakers first; then we'll go eat pizza."

They were on the way to the car when Jacqueline's cell phone chirped. It was Jeff. "Hi, Jeff. Did you find out anything new?"

"Can you talk?" he asked in a serious tone.

"I'm with the kids right now."

"So you know the girl you asked me about last night, Reyna—"

"Is she the same Reyna?" Jacqueline interrupted, holding her breath in anticipation.

"Yes, Phil's girlfriend died a couple of days ago in a car accident."

"Jesus," said Jacqueline, stunned. "I expected to hate her for breaking up my marriage, but I feel terrible."

"That's not all."

"What do you mean? Is Phil okay?"

"Yes," said Jeff, "but there's more to the story. Call me when you get home."

Jacqueline agreed and immediately called Ariana, who was just arriving at her destination in New Jersey for her business meeting.

"Hey, darling! Miss me already?" teased Ariana.

"Ari, the girl at the funeral home really was Phil's girlfriend."

"Holy crap!" Ariana squawked in surprise. "That's karma, honey."

"Don't talk like that, Ari. I feel horrible for her parents, her family. She was so young—"

"Don't you feel bad for what happened to that girl! You had nothing to do with her death." Ariana sounded calm despite being no less surprised than Jacqueline. Jacqueline told her that Jeff had more news but hadn't wanted to give her the details in front of the boys.

"Geez. So he's saving the good stuff for later . . . so typical," Ariana griped as she gazed around the lobby of an apartment building that was almost as luxurious as Jacqueline's.

"I'll see you at the apartment in a little bit," said Jacqueline and ended the call.

Ariana stepped into the elevator. On the designated floor, she knocked at the door of the couple's apartment, and a moment later a tall, voluptuous woman answered. She greeted Ariana with a broad smile.

"Hello," she said. "I'm Martha. Welcome." She led Ariana into the spacious living room. Ariana followed, appreciating the sophisticated white furniture and the simple lamps that hung from the enviably high ceilings.

"You have a beautiful apartment," said Ariana.

"Thank you. We have a few other units here, but we use this one to host family gatherings or guests from out of town. It's so conveniently close to the city."

Their conversation floated lightly from the weather to the beautiful neighborhood around the building to children and school styles nowadays.

Ariana accepted a glass of water, and the moment the lady returned to her seat, she opted to get right to the point.

"I had a talk with the other investors in this building, and it seems they all agree about converting the building to condos. Your husband seems to be the only holdout. Why?" Ariana asked bluntly.

The lady shook her head. "Well, he likes to keep things simple. He feels that rentals are always more profitable. If he converts the building into condos for sale, he'll be able to collect only a lump sum, with no long-term earnings."

"It wouldn't be such a bad idea to sell," Ariana said. "The market would be in your favor. It's a seller's market right now."

"I wouldn't mind selling, but my husband has the final say."

"Do you think he would reconsider for the right price?" Ariana asked while jotting a few notes in her yellow notepad.

"Perhaps," said Martha. "He does have plenty of other business on his plate right now. He might be willing if the price is right. There you are!" she said as her husband walked into the living room from the outside terrace.

Ariana rose from her seat, eager to meet him. As she looked up and extended her hand, her eyes bulged in disbelief. William, the man she had gone to bed with and sent to the hospital only a few nights prior, now stood in front of her. He stared back at her with equal astonishment and turned as pale as the pristine furniture in the place. His wife, Martha, carried on, wholly oblivious to their reactions.

"This is my husband, William," she said nonchalantly.

Ariana glanced back at Martha as he reached for her hand. After a moment of silence, Ariana turned her focus back to him with a forced smile. "Good afternoon to you, sir. Have we met?" she asked with noticeable sarcasm.

William shook his head in denial. His wife, however, had detected the sudden flow of tense energy between them.

"Do you know each other?" she asked, frowning.

"No! Not at all!" Ariana interrupted in a casual tone. "I thought for a second . . . but I guess your husband has one of those familiar faces, you know . . ."

William retreated to the kitchen for a glass of water and reappeared wearing a coy smile, a thin mask over his nervousness.

"I don't believe we have," he said. "William Harron. It's a pleasure." His tone was even more formal than usual.

"The pleasure is all mine."

Martha's cell phone rang. "Excuse me, ma'am," she said. "It's my eldest son. He just moved to his college campus a few days ago. I'll be right back."

Ariana nodded as Martha walked into the next room.

"You have been such a waste of my time—" Ariana started in, indignant.

"Are you stalking me? What the hell are you doing here?" William demanded defensively.

"Stalking you? Oh, please. Don't flatter yourself." Ariana snatched her purse from the coffee table. "I haven't thought of you for a fraction of a second since you left in that ambulance. And as it turns out, you *are* married! Surprise, surprise . . ."

"I owe you no explanation whatsoever," he said.

Ariana chuckled bitterly. "Really? I don't need any! But I think your wife probably does," she whispered.

Ariana had the upper hand; there was no way around it. He had been dishonest about his marriage and current living situation, and life had played a fair turn to put him in his place. Ariana was fiery and relentless and would not think twice about exposing him to his wife. William struggled to rein in his composure and grasped for the right words to placate Ariana.

"Let's talk about this elsewhere. Not here. I think it's better if you leave . . ." William said, his facade crumbling. His face was pale and his hands trembled. He could not believe his luck with Ariana and was starting to suspect she was part of some strange plot to make his life hell on earth.

Ariana stepped into the hallway, then turned to stare at him with piercing eyes. "You won't get off the hook that easy," she said, waving her finger in his face. "You have twenty-four hours to sign the proposal for the condo conversion."

"I won't, and I won't be blackmailed into it." His resolve returned instantly.

Ariana rummaged in her purse for an envelope, from which she plucked an invoice. "You most certainly will," she said, flashing the ambulance invoice with his information. "Because if you don't, well, let's just say you might end up with more expenses other than the few hundred dollars in this ambulance bill. How about we pass it on to your wife? Does she sign the checks?" she threatened.

"That won't be necessary," he said, his bravado fizzling. Just then, he jolted at the presence of his wife. She had finished her call and was now watching Ariana, who stood in the doorway.

"Well, is everything okay?" she asked. "What did I miss?"

"We're good," William said, handing Ariana his business card. "If you're the realtor assigned by the investment group, make sure you send me the proposal. My email address is on the card."

William's wife turned from Ariana to William, seemingly confused. He explained that he had agreed to consider the proposal. Perhaps the condo conversion would be a good idea after all and the sum that he earned from the transaction could help cover for a new business venture. She was speechless at his sudden change of heart. Ariana noticed her demeanor and smiled.

"I think your husband understands that it's in his best interest to let his partners turn this building into a condo conversion. We agreed that the deal would be favorable from a financial standpoint. Besides, we are sure the transaction will help lift some incredible weight off his shoulders."

"Well, that's news to me," said Martha. They stood side by side as Ariana opened the door to leave.

"Since we understand each other now, I think it's best that I email you the documents in the morning."

"I'll have my attorney review them sometime next week," he confirmed.

"Perfect! It was so very nice to meet you both!" Ariana said cheerfully. "Goodbye, now!"

The unexpected blow had turned out to be a blessing in disguise. Since her attorney friend's office was nearby, Ariana called him and they agreed to discuss her divorce case over coffee and lunch.

Ariana had recounted her history with William prior to their impromptu meeting. Her attorney friend remembered William from when his car had been towed and he had given him a lift from the courthouse to the impound. He snickered at Ariana's anecdotes and confessed that he viewed her as a very unique individual. Ariana's bluntness had served as a hard lesson for William, who would surely quit the bar scene, at least for a while.

"How is it that so many married men are such lying bastards? Their audacity is impressive!"

Her friend nodded, holding in his laughter. "Most men cheat," he admitted. "Especially the ones with above-average incomes. I don't mean to stereotype, but they do." He handed a few bills to the server.

"Why do you think that is?" Ariana asked.

"They have the resources that lead to more opportunities, I guess."

"It's funny how, most of the time, women are the ones who pressure the man into marriage, and we're usually the first to turn and file for divorce," she commented. "I'll never bother getting married again. There's no point."

"You're right!" he said. "Nine times out of ten, it's the woman who files for divorce—I see it all the time."

"But why do you think that is?" she asked.

"Because men like the stability of a home life, but at the same time we also like to conquer. I think hunting for acceptance from the opposite sex is wired into our DNA. We can love our wives but still cheat if the opportunity arises." He pulled his cell phone from his pocket and called a car for Ariana.

"I really appreciate everything you've done for me," she said.

"Your divorce was relatively uncomplicated. Read the documents closely, and if you agree with the terms, sign them and bring them to the office. Carlos's attorney mentioned that once the documents are all signed, it should take only a couple of weeks to wrap everything up. He also said that Carlos wanted to give you an advance. He knows you have no money, and well, I pressured them to give you something up front. You should have a check in hand by Tuesday of next week. He's working on refinancing the house so he can pay you."

"Oh, thank God!" she sighed in relief. "I'll call you if I have any questions."

Ariana got into the black Lincoln Town Car to head back to the city, and her attorney watched from the sidewalk as the vehicle drove away.

She walked into Jacqueline's apartment and noted without surprise that Jacqueline had not yet made it home. She flopped down on the bed and read every word of the divorce papers. To her surprise, Carlos had offered more money for her share of the house. Ariana suspected that his generosity had something to do with his profoundly guilty conscience and his desire to send her off in the most harmonious way possible, given the circumstances.

Her eyes watered as she read the last document. As much as she wanted the divorce, the failure of her marriage was still a hard pill to swallow. She sat pensively, immersed in doubts about the role she had played for so many years. Had she ever been a good wife, whatever that was? Normal home life no longer existed in her life, and starting over in her mid-forties was an intimidating journey she felt far from ready to embark on.

Nevertheless, she realized she and her soon-to-be ex-husband had lost their connection long ago, and all that remained was the daily routine they perceived as a comfortable married life. The time she'd spent away from Carlos had served her well. It had broken the spell that kept her confined to the illusion, and now, she had the mental clarity that helped her realize she hadn't been living, only surviving in a loveless marriage.

Ariana signed the documents without a second thought. She knew she was doing the right thing for once and felt relieved. She was on the right track now and would enjoy everything she'd missed out on, living life the right way while learning to love herself and reconnecting with her son. That was what mattered the most.

A short time later, Jacqueline came home with the boys. Josefina's dog ran out of the room when he heard them coming, giving the apartment a delightful welcoming energy.

Ariana emerged from the bedroom, running to Jacqueline, clearly bursting with a secret. "Jacky, you won't believe who I saw today!" she whispered.

Jacqueline tossed her shopping bags onto the armchair in the foyer, watching her boys as they played on the floor with the dog.

"Boys! Go take a shower before dinner!" she called. "Let me get the boys in line first. They're driving me crazy." She pulled Mark's arm, prompting him to stand.

Phil Junior walked to his room, and Jacqueline led Mark to the bathroom and turned on the shower. She got their pajamas ready, and soon the boys were settled on the living room sofa, watching TV and waiting for dinner to be served. Jacqueline signaled for Ariana to follow her to her bedroom.

"Guess who the guy was." Ariana sat on Jacqueline's bed, unable to contain herself any longer.

"What guy?"

"Remember how I told you I had to meet with an investor in New Jersey?"

"Yes. Who was it?"

"William!" Ariana squealed and let out a hysterical laugh.

"I don't believe you!" said Jacqueline, amazed.

"And you know what? He's married!"

"But he said he was separated, remember?" said Jacqueline. "He never told us he was divorced."

"Well, he told me he was getting a divorce. He was at the apartment with his wife, and they didn't look separated at all—in fact, you should've seen his face when he saw me."

Jacqueline laughed. "Why am I not surprised? After what happened with you the other night, any man would be scared to death at the sight of you!"

"When his wife left the room to take a call, he begged me to leave. He was shitting bricks!"

Jacqueline laughed it off and reminded her friend what a difference a year alone would make to her. It would help her adjust to sober living, and she should stay single for a while whether William was married or single. Ariana agreed and told Jacqueline she had blackmailed William into signing the proposal by threatening to give his wife the ambulance bill and tell her about their encounters. Ariana was confident he wouldn't risk his marriage.

"Ariana, that's blackmail. You should be the bigger person." Jacqueline reprimanded her like a rebellious teenage daughter. "Be the bigger person!" she shouted again in William's defense.

Ariana turned at the end of the hallway with a broad smile. "Jacky, at this point in my life I don't give a rat's ass about being the bigger person. I have bills to pay and a job to get. Besides, I'm doing that scum a favor!"

"Really? How so?" Jacqueline called from the bathroom, undressing for a bath.

"Next time that jerk goes out to pick up chicks, he's going to think twice. He might even learn to appreciate the woman he has at home!"

Jacqueline peeked into the hallway at her with a knowing smile. Ariana went into her room, leaving Jacqueline alone to enjoy a hot bath.

Over half an hour had passed when Jacqueline stepped out of the tub and into her pajamas. Right when she was on her way to get dinner for the boys, Jeff called.

"Hang on, Jeff. Give me a sec," she said, stepping into the kitchen. Ariana was already there, serving herself some pasta, and Jacqueline asked her to serve the children as well. She had to take Jeff's call and had no idea how long she might be. Josefina, who had arrived only a few minutes before, helped Ariana set the table.

Back in her bedroom, Jacqueline closed the door and sat on her bed.

"I'm back," she said. "What's going on? What did you find out?"

"Well, it seems Reyna was not the devoted girlfriend Phil thought she was."

"What do you mean?" Jacqueline asked in suspense.

"Did you know that Phil bought an apartment in her name?"

"What?" gasped Jacqueline, in shock. "What apartment? Where?"

"Phil bought her an apartment in Gramercy Park," he said firmly.

"In his name or hers? She couldn't possibly afford a place there, not even a rental! Not with what she made in Phil's office, anyway."

"I don't think I'm making myself clear, Jacky," he tried again. "He bought the apartment in her name but signed for the mortgage. They were planning to move in together when your divorce was finalized. In the meantime, Reyna had already put the apartment up for sale without telling him."

"How? Why would she do that?" Jacqueline asked in a cold voice.

"Phil had put down more than six hundred thousand dollars. If she sold it, she would get at least that much in closing."

"Phil put that much money down on a property in her name? Is he insane?"

"Apparently so. He just found out the place had been on the market for a month and that Reyna had another boyfriend. She was planning to sell the apartment and use the cash to start a new life with the other guy."

"How would you know that?"

"I could only get the number for Reyna's aunt. I called to offer my condolences. She was a close friend of the boyfriend's mother. She was quite chatty. I didn't invest too much effort to find out the details."

"What happens now? Can we sell the apartment in Gramercy?" asked Jacqueline.

"The apartment will go to Reyna's family. Phil can't claim it; he's not on the title as an owner, only as a grantor for the loan, so all the money he sank into that place, thousands of dollars, it's all down the drain," said Jeff.

"But that was my money, too!"

"Yes, but now we can claim that amount as part of his share of the assets. Anyway, they both had life insurance on the mortgage, so the girl's family will get the property debt-free. Maybe Phil's attorney can work something out with her family. Whatever he put toward that apartment was yours too, so we can use that in your favor, I'm sure."

"I could kill him right now," she sighed.

"Phil is a mess, Jacky. He feels like a fool."

"With good reason!" she shouted. "Was she even planning to marry him?"

"Jacqueline, I already told you," Jeff said. "Reyna put the apartment up for sale to take the money and run away with that other guy."

"She was seeing another guy?" It finally dawned on her. "He was probably in on it, too."

"Yes, but I still don't know how she managed to hide her double life from Phil."

"Oh, trust me," Jacqueline retorted in a know-it-all tone, "the person who gets cheated on is usually the last to find out. Been there."

"I guess you're right," said Jeff with a sigh.

Jacqueline still cared enough about Phil that it grieved her to see him humiliated to such a degree. She struggled with her own emotions, and for a moment, she thought that perhaps the experience would change Phil into the man she wished he had been. If only she could let go of her resentment and overlook his past shortcomings and evil ways.

"How is Phil?" Jacqueline asked with compassion. He was, after all, the father of her children. They had spent over twenty-five years together, much of it good.

"He wants to see you," said Jeff. "He told me this afternoon that he would like to speak with you in person."

"I don't think I'm ready for that yet." Her heart shrank in pain.

"I think he wants a second chance, Jacky. He didn't say that explicitly, but I know he feels deeply ashamed."

"He should," said Jacqueline. "Should I meet him in your office? Did you show him the list I gave you?" she asked, feeling overwhelmed with doubts—second thoughts about her divorce.

"Let me call him first. Should I tell him you'll meet him? Outside my office, I mean? In case he asks?"

"Of course, Jeff. Of course I would."

"I'll call you in the morning," he said. They wished each other a good night.

Jacqueline went to check on the boys, and it warmed her heart to see them on the sofa with Josefina's dog. Josefina went to her room and packed up the few things she had left. Jacqueline tucked the boys into bed and joined Ariana in front of the TV. Josefina sat with them as well, and the three of them talked and laughed together at Ariana's jokes and her recounting of her meeting with William.

Josefina had been right all along—William was married. They all agreed that when a man had a clean conscience and good intentions, he had no need to be secretive.

"They're terrible at lying," said Josefina.

"You're right," said Jacqueline. "Sometimes we think it's easier to ignore the red flags and pretend everything's fine."

Ariana nodded. "True. I guess it's so much easier to believe what they say, at least in the beginning—"

"The beginning is the most important!" Josefina interrupted. "If you ignore those red flags when you're only dating, who knows? You might be too invested later and believe anything. We women can be silly that way sometimes."

Josefina was not very religious but explained her belief that a greater power, more likely than not, used situations to bring people together and that everything unfolded at the right time and place, for reasons people only understood much later. Jacqueline agreed that there were no coincidences. Ariana, too, shared her certainty that life events would always somehow either teach people a lesson or humble them, and sometimes both.

It had been an interesting day, and though their backgrounds differed in every way, they had to agree that when it came to life's challenges and everyday lessons, there was little difference between them. The pain of betrayal and separation tended to be equal and, to all, the same.

Chapter 13

Josefina rose early the next morning to find the apartment feeling cozier than usual. Jacqueline's children had transformed the energy of the place in less than a day. Josefina gathered her belongings and placed them in the foyer. She had only the backpack that she carried daily and now, thanks to Jacqueline, a large suitcase. She considered knocking on Jacqueline's bedroom door before getting ready but refrained, conscious of their late bedtime the night before.

If Jacqueline had not awakened by the time she was ready to leave, she would leave a thank-you note in a place where she would find it. With that in mind, Josefina enjoyed a warm shower and got dressed in minutes. When she walked into the living room, ready to go, she caught the scent of fresh coffee and went straight to the kitchen.

"Good morning!" said Jacqueline. She had been up for a while, unbeknownst to Josefina, and had brewed the coffee while Josefina took her shower.

"Good morning, Jacky." Josefina poured herself a cup of coffee and followed Jacqueline to the dining room table. "I have to get my dog out of the children's room, but I'm afraid I'll wake them."

"Will your new employer allow you to keep Nono while you're living there?" asked Jacqueline.

"Yes. I already asked about that," said Josefina in a low voice. "But I don't know how long I'll be able to. Hopefully they don't give me trouble about the issue once I'm there."

Jacqueline nodded. "I can imagine. I'll be right back," said Jacqueline. She stood and went to get the puppy. Her children had taken a real liking to Josefina's dog, and she knew that Mark especially would complain about having the puppy taken away. When Jacqueline entered the room, Nono started barking and woke the boys. Soon after she returned to the table, they stumbled groggily into the dining room and joined her for breakfast. Mark sat on the floor, playing with the puppy, while Phil Junior poured a bowl of cereal. By then, Ariana, too, had risen and sat down next to Jacqueline, wrapped in her warm fuchsia bathrobe.

"Are you excited about your new job?" Ariana asked Josefina, who was gathering her dog's food, toys, and snacks into a plastic bag.

"Yes! It's such a relief to me. Being far from the city, at least for a while, will do me some good. The pay is much better too, compared to what I used to make."

"I'm sure you'll do great," said Jacqueline. Josefina nodded in agreement.

"You girls have done so much for me. I'll owe you for the rest of my life!" Josefina said. Ariana rubbed her shoulder affectionately.

"You've done a lot for us, too. If there's ever anything you need, please know that you can count on me," said Jacqueline. Little Mark carried on playing with the dog, refusing to let Josefina leave with him even though she had already hooked the leash to his collar. Josefina tugged coaxingly on the leash, but Mark simply would not let go of the dog he had already come to view as a fixture of the house.

"Enough, Mark," Jacqueline reprimanded.

"Mom! It's not fair!" he argued. Josefina stood by the door, waiting for the boy to let go. But when she noticed that Nono kept pulling away from her, she realized that he, too, had grown to love the children and the new place. Josefina leaned toward Jacqueline and laid a hand on her arm.

"Jacky, I really don't know how long I'll be able to keep Nono with me. At my new job, I mean," she whispered. "Your boys love him. I wouldn't want to impose, but would you like to keep him?" Her eyes nearly betrayed her doubt about the offer she had just made, and she had no idea what to expect.

"I wouldn't dare," Jacqueline said with mixed feelings. "They've never had a dog. Trust me, they'll be just fine without one." As the words left her lips, she realized that a pet in the house could prove soothing for her sons, who would soon face a challenging phase in their parents' divorce. Perhaps the puppy's presence could help comfort them amid the changes, deviating attention from the conflict.

"I'll be starting nursing school next year," said Josefina. "I'll have to give him to some other family, eventually, since I won't have much time to take care of him. Nothing would make me happier than to leave him with you. Of course, there's no pressure," Josefina said, crouching in the doorway to pet the puppy.

"Please, Mom!" begged the youngest one. "We'll take care of Nono better than anyone else would. Right, Phil?"

Phil Junior chimed in. "Mom! Why can't we keep him?"

At the thought of Nono's continued presence, the children were ecstatic, and their happiness radiated from their eyes. Jacqueline felt for the first time that she had the power to please them by making this decision without her husband's consent, and the thought was liberating. Mark tugged on her robe.

"Yes? Mom! Dad can't forbid us from having a dog if he's moving out . . ." Phil Junior thought aloud.

Jacqueline looked at them thoughtfully, and Ariana jumped in as their accomplice.

"C'mon, Jacky. Lighten up! I think a pet could help them adjust to the changes. Studies show that pets are helpful when kids are dealing with traumatic situations. Now that you're divorcing, I think it would be a great idea to replace one dog with a better one!" said Ariana jokingly.

Jacqueline looked at her sons' faces as they stared back at her with eyes full of hope. She smiled. "Okay. We'll keep him. But I want you guys to take care of him, and I mean it. You have to bathe him and look after him, feed him—everything. Understood?" The kids jumped excitedly, hugging her. The realization was growing inside of her; now she would have a chance to establish new rules and bond freely with her boys without Phil's scrutiny, and that alone made her swell with pride.

"I, too, have a condition before I give Nono away," said Josefina. The children were lying on the floor with the dog and looked up at her, listening attentively. "I want you to let me come see him now and then. Deal?" She stood holding the door open with one hand, her suitcase in the other.

They nodded with big eyes and broad smiles.

Josefina let go of the leash. Mark wasted no time unhooking it from Nono's collar and carrying him to the living room. Josefina and Jacqueline had a short candid talk. Jacqueline had spoken to Jeff about Josefina's divorce. Jeff assured her that it would be less complicated than she expected, and that given Josefina's financial situation, as a favor to Jacqueline, he would be glad to help and would charge her only for the administrative and court costs. He would be there whenever she was ready. Jacqueline and Josefina hugged, and Josefina left. Ariana joined Phil Junior and Mark to watch TV.

Jacqueline cleaned up the table and went to take a shower before starting her day. Donna arrived shortly afterward. It was Sunday, but she would be there to work half a day. Ariana helped her in the kitchen, suggesting they cook something new for the children. After asking the kids what they would like, they opted for pizza, which made the chore much simpler for Donna. Ariana assured her she would call in the order sometime later. It was not yet noon.

That rainy Sunday morning, the streets of the big city were dark. It was an ideal day for lounging around the house and watching movies. The boys decided on Batman, and even Ariana enjoyed sitting with them as a family. They had just started the second movie when the home phone rang. It was Jeff. Jacqueline picked up the phone and walked to her bedroom, closing the door for privacy.

"Hi, Jeff. Anything new? Did you talk to Phil?" Jacqueline asked in suspense.

"Yes. He wants to see you for lunch today—but only if you want to."

"Today? But I just sat down with the children."

"All right, no worries. I'll tell him you're busy. He can see you at my office next week."

"No! No!" she interrupted, having second thoughts. "Tell him I'll meet him. I'd rather get our last talk over with. Besides, some alone time might be just what we need before we decide how to split our assets. He's been through a lot, and I feel horrible about it. Where does he want to meet?" Jacqueline wanted the opportunity to connect with the father of her children, if only for a few minutes, before writing off her marriage entirely.

"He would like to treat you to Le Cirque at one o'clock. I'll tell him right now if you're willing to meet."

Jacqueline looked at the clock on her bedside table. It was already twelve fifteen.

"Tell him I'll see him there."

"All right, then," said Jeff.

"Jeff!" Jacqueline said excitedly.

"Yes?"

"Le Cirque is my favorite restaurant. Phil and I celebrated our wedding anniversary there for the past seven years."

"I know," Jeff replied. "I hope a good meal and a long talk can help you guys develop some conflict resolution skills. If you need anything, just call. You know how it is," he said, sounding more like a protective older brother than a lawyer.

Jacqueline passed the news on to Ariana. They agreed not to say anything to the boys about Jacqueline's lunch with Phil. After all, Jacqueline was not sure why Phil wanted to see her, let alone how she would feel afterward.

The boys stayed home with Ariana and Nono. They were content to watch their movie and unmotivated to ask their mother any questions. Jacqueline put on a little makeup and styled her loose wavy hair. She threw on a long black dress with a cotton shrug and high-heeled boots that made her look like a magazine model rather than a depressed and neglected wife.

Given the dull and rainy weather that afternoon, Jacqueline chose to take a taxi to the restaurant. It was surprisingly busy for a Sunday. She gave her information to the hostess, who immediately escorted her to Phil's table. He was impeccably dressed, as usual, in a pair of jeans and a black cashmere turtleneck sweater that he complemented with a beige wool and silk jacket.

Phil rose from his chair, and they greeted each other awkwardly, like a couple on a blind date. He seemed nervous and looked exhausted, with unusually dark bags under his eyes. For a moment, she wanted to believe that his tired fragility was due to the toll that their separation had taken. Deep inside, however, she knew to attribute his condition to the loss of his girlfriend as well as the shock of learning about her deception.

"How are you, Phil?" she asked gently, sounding genuinely concerned.

"I'm doing all right. How are you?" said Phil, absorbed in the lunch menu. He couldn't look her in the eyes.

"I'm doing much better now that I have my boys back," said Jacqueline, perusing the menu. Phil sensed a note of sarcasm in her voice and lowered the menu to the table, next to his plate.

"Please, Jacky, let's not start like this," he said. "I told Jeff that I wanted to see you for a good reason."

Jacqueline was well aware of his drama. He was under the impression that Jacqueline had no idea about Reyna's dirty laundry and knew only about her death.

"I'm sorry about Reyna," Jacqueline said.

Phil took a sip from his wine glass and looked up at her. He was not surprised that Jacqueline knew Reyna had died.

"Who told you? Jeff, I assume."

"Yes. He only told me because you canceled our meetings at his office several times. I asked him what was wrong, so he told me. That's all," she said nonchalantly.

"Thank you, Jacky. It's been a shock for all of us at the office."

"I'm truly sorry, for you and for her family," Jacqueline said, then turned her attention to the waiter as he made his speech about the special of the day. She ordered an appetizer and some iced tea. Phil reached for her hand.

"Jacky," he said, "Reyna and I had many problems. I don't know how to tell you this, but . . . since I left home, I've been thinking about you and the boys."

"Look, Phil," Jacqueline said, "I don't want to hear it. It took you thirty days and the loss of your lover for you to think of your family? Thanks for keeping us in second and third place. Some things will never change." She turned away in disgust.

"Actually, it's not like that, Jacky. I think I made a mistake," said Phil, resting his hand on her lap.

Jacqueline lifted his hand from her leg gently and placed it on the table. She picked up her glass, sipping her iced tea mostly out of nervousness. His approach confused her; from her perspective, their meeting at this place was not to celebrate but to achieve formal closure. Phil smiled at her, and his worn-out countenance exposed his drowning soul. For the first time, she felt detached, and to her surprise, being able to trust his word no longer mattered to her.

Jacqueline thought about the last few years of their life together and realized it was not their marriage he wanted to preserve but his image. He had been humiliated by his deceased mistress and would now have to face that shame alone.

She looked him straight in the eye. "What is it you want, Phil?"

"I want us to be a family again, Jacqueline," he said. He sounded sincere. "I'm not proud of what I've done, but everyone deserves a second chance, Jacky. We should try to keep our family together, for our kids' sake, and for us too. I hope you can find it in your heart to give me one more chance."

Jacqueline was silent. She felt weak before him for a moment, but that changed quickly as a sudden sense of pride gave her the emotional strength she had lacked for so many years. She was overwhelmed by the kind of courage that only a profound determination to maintain one's sanity could bring. She patted his hand, then withdrew hers. This time she did it with a firm stare and not so gently.

"Really?" Jacqueline said, and Phil nodded with a half-smile.

Jacqueline looked down as the waiter filled their glasses with water. When he was gone, she smiled. Phil leaned closer, pulling his chair next to hers.

"Jacky, I know we can be happy. We can go to couples therapy like you always wanted—whatever you think is necessary," he said encouragingly.

Jacqueline watched him hope with hardened eyes, and she wanted to believe him. Her new sense of self-respect and newly acquired independence told her that she now faced a crossroads. She imagined her future. Her new life had changed her outlook and allowed her to breathe again. Her daily focus was now on finding herself, and she was enjoying the process. That sense of self and her children were all she could think of now. She wouldn't go back to relive her last years with Phil. He would have made changes a long time ago if he truly cared.

"I'm sorry, Phil. I think it's a little late to rekindle our burned-out relationship."

"What do you mean? We've only been separated for thirty days, Jacky. Some people go longer than that and work it out just fine," said Phil, almost begging.

"No, Phil. We haven't been separated for thirty days; we've been separated for the past ten years, thanks to you. We were just sharing the same roof, and I was blind. But now I can see what would happen if I gave you another chance. Sure, we'd be cozy for a few months, until you met some other girl like Reyna and made your kids and me go through hell all over again."

"Don't talk like that, Jacky."

"Yes, Phil, I will talk like that," she said as she rose from her chair.

"You left home. You used our money to buy property for someone who didn't give a rat's ass about you, and now that you're humiliated, you actually expect me to take you back and go on as if nothing happened?" said Jacqueline, grabbing her purse.

"But I told you I'm willing to go to couples therapy," said Phil, barely above a whisper.

"I suggested that years ago, but you were too busy having fun. Now it's my turn. I want to be with my children, and when I'm not with them, I'm going to go out and have a life. I want to have fun, too!" she said.

"So, you're saying you prefer to be alone? Like an old maid?" said Phil, the mask lifting to reveal his familiar vicious arrogance.

Jacqueline raised her hand to summon the waiter. "My coat, please," she said, and the young man went to retrieve her mink coat.

"Don't do this, Jacqueline. You're acting like an irrational, spoiled child!" Phil said, almost clenching his teeth. The other customers were watching from their tables.

"No, Phil. I'm not a spoiled child. I was only an idiot for staying with you after you made it clear that our marriage was over years ago," she said, pulling her coat on.

"If you walk away now, you'll regret it," said Phil.

Jacqueline calmly slipped her hands into her black leather gloves. "Do you know what I regret?" she asked, hooking her bag over her shoulder. "Staying with you. You have a nice lunch. My attorney will be contacting you soon." She felt the spirit of her brand-new self as she walked calmly out of the place with square shoulders and a confident smile.

Phil signaled the waiter and asked for the bill.

For the first time in years, Jacqueline breathed the scent of self-respect and was not the least bit intimidated by Phil's childish threats. She was a new woman and knew that only a healthy self-esteem could give her the independence that would forever be her best ally. She would make goals for herself and live to love her family and friends, and Phil would not be one of them.

Within minutes, Jacqueline was taking off her coat in her apartment, and Ariana ran to meet her.

"Guess what? William signed the agreement. What a jerk."

"Well, what does that mean for you now? Aren't you supposed to get a position with that new development project?"

"Yes!" Ariana's eyes sparkled. "I just spoke to my new boss. They're giving me the contract for a sales position, and once I've sold the first five units, they'll promote me to sales manager for their preconstruction project downtown!"

"Congratulations!" Jacqueline said, thrilled at her friend's success.

Ariana followed her to the bedroom. "So how was your lunch with Phil?"

"I ordered, and I let him talk . . . but only for a few minutes," said Jacqueline as she sat on the bed to remove her tall boots.

Ariana frowned. "But you didn't even spend an hour with him!"

"No, and I left behind a full plate of food."

"Why didn't you eat?"

"I realized I wasn't hungry," said Jacqueline with a broad smile.

"So you didn't eat . . ."

Jacqueline shook her head. "Seeing his face simply turned my stomach. I lost my appetite," she said and shrugged.

Ariana and Jacqueline shared a laugh and went back to sit with the boys in the living room. The boys cuddled with Jacqueline on the couch, devouring a bowl of popcorn. She was enjoying her children more than ever before, and she knew then that she would be a mother first and foremost. Dating would be nowhere on the horizon in the near future, and anything unrelated to her children or building her self-worth would have to wait.

Ariana managed to reach her son, Charley, and arranged to meet him within the week, after he finished his exams. Ariana and Jacqueline now had something in common: the determination to build a new life.

Jacqueline was unsure of what to expect regarding the financial settlement, and after seeing just how adept Phil could be at throwing money away, she was quite concerned. However, watching Josefina overcome her financial struggles in a foreign country on her path to the triumph of her well-earned accomplishments had inspired Jacqueline. She knew that no matter what life threw at her, she would be ready to overcome any challenge.

She was now in the process of getting to know her new self and would enjoy the ride. After all, she had her two growing boys and herself to think about and build a future for. Regardless of her insecurities, Jacqueline had learned that change was a process, and, it would always be better to take it one day at a time. She was off to a good start.

The End

SINGULAR A PUBLISING LLC

www.ingramcontent.com/pod-product-compliance
Lightning Source LLC
Chambersburg PA
CBHW022124170626
46808CB00002B/824